IF I FALL

à novel

Jeni,
Happy Reading!
Kelseyleigh Reber

Kelseyleigh Reber

If I Fall

1
WATCHING

Frothy waves claw at the shore, reaching for the unattainable, reaching for me. The murky blue mixes with a mysterious sea green in an endless mesh of wave on wave. The moon, a luminous white disk, glistens. Beckoning me forward, the man in the moon calls to me. Ferocious wind and powerless sand dance a waltz around my ankles, stinging my legs. Squinting through the hazy night, I watch as jagged rocks slice through the water.

Sea salt rests on the tip of my tongue, bitter and briny. I lick my chapped lips, but the taste remains. Silence echoes all around me. The waves crash closer and closer, the icy water seeping into the sand under my feet and caressing my toes. It wraps a cool hand around my ankle, pulling me closer. The frigid sea runs through my veins like arctic slush as I succumb to the power of Poseidon.

I am aware of all of this and yet, I feel nothing.

Mindlessly, I wade into the water. The waves push me back. I move closer—two steps forward, one step back—

until the waves lap at my waist. My dress floats on top of the water, bubbling out around me. The corset's tight ties deprive me of air, but hard as I try, I cannot free myself of its clutches. I am too exhausted, numbed by the night's events.

Hollow screams carry across the water, making my skin crawl. Glancing behind me, I see my sister sitting on the beach, her back turned to me as she gazes into the distance. Her light blonde hair cascades down her back and around her shoulders. She does not look at me; she is unable to tear her eyes away from the entrancing and terrifying view.

The sky is on fire; hot reds and oranges burn on the horizon. Smoke envelops the stars in a blanket of fog, shielding them from the horrors below. A high-pitched scream sounds in the night. Another follows it, and I tense. Could that be my mother's cry? My father's? I watch as our village burns and the wails of those I knew mix with another explosion.

My sister looks back at me, her tear-streaked cheeks glistening in the moonlight. I try to muster a smile, but can only manage a weak grimace. Slowly, I walk back to the beach. The waves egg me on, pushing at my back. I stumble onto the sand, a wave knocking me off balance, and sit beside my sister.

Grains of sand adhere to my slick skin, but I don't bother trying to wipe them off. I gaze down at her, so young and confused. Her glassy blue eyes peer up at me and she sniffles.

"I'm afraid," she whispers.

"Me too, Dela," I whisper back. "Me too."

She scoots closer, nuzzling her head into my shoulder. "Do you think Mother and Father will be all right?"

"Yes. They will find us in America just as they promised, you'll see," I lie.

Her nose runs and she wipes it on her sleeve. I begin to chide her, but think better of it. Besides, what does it really matter anymore?

"And you believe we will make it to America?"

"We shall make it. On my life, I promise you, we shall make it if it kills me."

Dela winces, pulling away. "Don't say such things. It's not so funny anymore."

She is right. Death is too set in reality to be humorous now, especially with our parents still caught in the village. My heart aches with grief as I watch the only home I have ever known burn in the distance.

"I do not want to go to America. Dianne said the people there are awfully rude," Dela says.

"We don't have a choice. America is where they are sending the refugees—"

"Yes, but not our people," she argues. "There are no ships to take us."

"We will find a way. We have no other choice. Liverpool

is no longer safe, not for us."

"I still don't wish to leave," she grumbles.

I grab her hands and make her look me in the eyes. "If you wish to live, Dela, then you will leave with me. We can never come back, not while the war is going on."

She nods, returning her gaze to the fiery skies. "Not ever," she whispers. "Our home has been destroyed."

With that said, Dela leans closer and we both look to the glowing sky, knowing that just below lies a ruined village. I cradle her in my arms as we listen to the waves crash behind us and the cries of our beloved rising towards the heavens like burning embers caught on the wind.

2
FLEEING

Two hours earlier...

"Elvira! Wake up!" My mother's urgent whispers wake me with a start. Groggy and half asleep, I get out of bed. Too fast. My head whirls and my sight goes fuzzy. I put a hand to my head until it clears. The hardwood floors are cold against my bare feet and a breeze passes through my thin nightdress. A sharp bang echoes from outside as a cloud of dust coughs up through the open window. Panicked, I reel on my mother.

"What is it? What is happening?" I ask.

She doesn't answer. "Get dressed, darling. Quickly."

I stare at the woman who brought me into this world. I stare at her and cannot help but remember the last time I saw her cry. I stare at her and realize that the last time I saw her cry was... never. My mother does not cry. Ever. And yet the tear that rolls down her cheek says otherwise.

"Dela. Dela, sweetheart, wake up," Mother says. My sister stirs, groaning, before rolling to the other side and letting her eyes flutter shut. "Dela, you must get out of bed!" Pulling at her arms, Mother finally gets Dela to her feet. Our bedroom's blue shadows cast over my sister's face, her net of golden hair failing to suppress the darkness. She rubs at her eyes, thoroughly annoyed.

"It's the middle of the night," she whines.

Mother ignores her complaining, moving towards our dresser. Hurriedly, she picks out a dress for Dela and helps her put it on. Frightened by the look on my mother's face, I do as she says and get dressed. A loud boom makes the house shudder and my fear grows. My hands fumble at my back.

"Blasted corset!" I yell, tempted to just forget it, but knowing I cannot. Even if all of Hell broke loose, my mother would not allow me to leave this house without a corset. It simply isn't proper! she would say; there was no point in arguing.

Mother leaves Dela to do the dress's buttons herself and with shaking hands ties the corset tight around my waist, making sure breathing is not an option. I feel her fingers scrabble along my back, their icy tips sending electric currents thrumming beneath my skin.

"Mother, please. Tell us. What is happening?"

Her pale eyes flit between the two of us with such a solemn intensity that my heart sinks before the words even escape her mouth.

"The village is under attack."

"By whom?" Dela gasps.

The crow's feet around Mother's eyes appear to deepen as she steps towards my bed. I used to associate those lines with the precious smiles I once believed to be rare gifts. When they gathered around her crystalline eyes, I knew I was receiving a special treat, my mother's approval. But now, as she traces a hand over my tattered quilt as though it is the last time she will ever see it again, I know that those lines suddenly have a very different meaning. Gone are the lines of happiness and laughter. Worry and terror—that is what I now see in the contours of her face. Two simple words and yet all-powerful. Worry and terror.

"The Radicals," she finally answers, ripping her hand back from the quilt as though it has unexpectedly turned to ash beneath her touch. She pushes by us, moving towards the bedroom door before whirling around to face us. "They are setting the whole village on fire. Your father is bringing the carriage around back. Are you both ready?"

We exchange withered glances and nod.

"Let's go, my darlings. Keep close, now."

We trail her down the stairs, through the kitchen, and out the back door. I glance back, wondering if it will be the last time I see my beloved home. Father pulls around in the coach. Two mares whinny and snort at the front, their nostrils flaring.

Jumping down from the perch, he runs around to aid Mother and Dela into the carriage. I stand behind them, unsure. Everything is moving so fast. Too fast. Only moments ago, I was lost in a dream, and now I am running for my life. My brain cannot process it all. Disbelief clouds my thoughts.

"Elvira! Come on!" my father calls.

Startled from my stupor, I turn and run to him, wanting him to hold me in his arms. I do not get his warm embrace, but rather a sharp push into the carriage. I stumble inside and take the seat opposite Mother and Dela. My skirts tangle around my legs as I turn in my seat to look out the back window.

Father snaps the reins and the carriage bustles into motion. The horses' fervent clip-clopping picks up tempo and the coach rocks back and forth. I watch my home grow smaller and smaller as we draw away. Another blast sounds through the air and I gasp. A plume of orange has sidled up the side of my house, leaving a trail of black in its wake.

Suddenly, my bedroom window bursts into a million shards of glass. They glint in the firelight as they rain down upon the soft grass. The flames sitting atop the roof lick at the cool night air as another window breaks with a thousand pings. Unable to watch any more, I face the front once again. We sit in silence, listening to our world go up in flames.

—

Mother covers Dela's ears, trying to protect her from the screams and cries around us. A green monster climbs up my stomach and I instantly push him back down. How silly of me to be jealous of my sister for being younger, for having Mother's warm hands wrapped around her ears. No, not so silly, really, to want someone to shield me from my fears. I wrap my arms around my waist, hugging myself. At the moment, I am all I have.

The carriage jostles and I am thrown roughly to the side. My shoulder bangs against the wall. Dela is thrust forward and Mother braces herself. I put a hand to my shoulder, trying to rub the ache out of it. My sister scrambles back onto the seat, her eyes wide with fear. We have stopped. The horses whinny.

"Whoa!" I hear my father yell, but the horses are wild with fright.

Another voice meets my father's and I tense. "Where you think you're going?"

The Radicals, I think, and my heartbeat quickens.

"We mean no harm. Please, just let us pass," Father says, his voice surprisingly calm.

I hear the man snicker. "Let you pass," he scoffs. "I say, show me your arm!"

"Please, sir. Let us be reasonable men."

"You are no man," he spits. "You aren't even human!

Now, show me your arm!"

Fear grips my heart with sharp claws and I can scarcely breathe. We are frozen, listening intently. What is happening out there?

"Let us pass," Father says. His voice is stern. It is the same voice he uses for scolding Dela and me, except this time I cannot escape to my room.

"Who you got back there?" the man says, and I can feel his cruel grin from inside the coach.

"No one," Father says, too quickly and the lie is evident. "It is just me."

"Pete, Ray, check the back."

Dela is crying now, tears streaming down her face in silent sobs. A hand grips my arm, fingernails digging deep into the flesh of my wrist. The hand pulls, slipping down around my fingers and squeezing. A shrill scream escapes my lips. I can feel my finger bones rub together beneath the skin and I fly out of the carriage, twisting my ankle. I bite my tongue to keep from crying out.

"Come along, poppet," my attacker whispers in my ear. His breath smells strongly of spirits and I wrinkle my nose. He pins my arms behind my back, my already cut and bruised wrist blistering in pain under the pressure of his grimy hands. He leads me to the front of the carriage.

The grunts and whimpers of Dela and Mother struggling against their captors reach me before I see them. Like me, they both have a Radical restraining their hands. It is hard to tell in the night, but something dark seems to stream from Mother's right ear and I can only assume it is blood. I cannot meet my father's eyes, but I know he is watching me.

"Please, let them go. They are not like me," he pleads.

"We'll see 'bout that," another man declares. He marches up to me, holding a knife. I try to back up, but the grip around my arms tightens. Around us, dark figures scurry and yells fly into the night, but they are in a different world. Separated by the circle of Radicals and far away from the nightmare I am living.

"Don't hurt her!" Father yells. He tries to run forward, but another Radical catches him by the shoulder, wrenching him down. Someone's knee jerks up with a resounding clap. Father falls back, rolling onto his stomach with a groan. He coughs. His lip is bloodied. A single eye begins to swell shut. It all happens so fast. A single yelp jumps from my tongue and falls unheard into the night.

The man looms closer, obscuring my view of Father and gagging me with the foul stench of spirits. Have all of these men been drinking? A cockamamie grin tugs at his lips. The few teeth left look as though they are decaying right before my eyes. I grimace, and his smile spreads.

"You a pretty one, all right. Can we save this one? Have a little fun before we kill 'er?" he jeers. His words are slurred, but they still have the same effect. My blood turns to ice and sweat forms on my lip and brow. Liquid fear.

He jerks my arm to him and his knife slips beneath my sleeve. The metal is cold against my skin, its razor sharp edge resting only inches from my vein. Blood thumps beneath the point. It races up my arm and pounds in my ears. I can feel it—hear it—thrumming against my skin, drowning out the mayhem around me.

With a swift twitch of the wrist, the dagger slices through my sleeve, exposing my bare forearm. My breath catches. On the creamy white of my arm there is a Mark, a perfect circle with a cross in the middle like a compass. It burns a bright violet, the same color as my eyes. He drops my arm and backs up. The man imprisoning my other arm sees the Mark and hastily releases his grasp. I stand between the two men, hopelessly frozen.

"What is it?" their leader calls, jumping down from the coach's perch. An explosion erupts behind us and we duck. A storm of debris showers over us; a fragment cuts across my cheek. Warm liquid bubbles to the surface and I press a finger to it. Hot and sticky, my finger is painted in a deep crimson. Wincing, I lean forward.

The explosion does not intimidate the Radicals. The leader continues to move forward, closing in fast. I catch a glimpse of his face in the flickering light of the battle raging around us. A long scar mars his features, threading across his cheek and over his lips. His eyes are a deep brown that appears black in the night.

"What is it?" he asks again. When no one answers, he grabs hold of my elbow and pulls me to him. He turns my arm in the night, this way and that. The Mark flares a brilliant violet in the firelight. His narrowed eyes widen, and he releases his hold in disgust. "What are your powers?" he bellows.

"I—I don't know."

He slaps me across the face. Hard. "Don't you lie to me!"

"Please. She speaks the truth. We don't know her powers," Father calls. "We don't believe she has any," he lies.

"She has the Circle and Cross! Do not play me for a fool! I know what the symbol means!"

I shudder with fear. My cheek stings with the imprint of his hand. What will happen to me? The Radical's suggestive taunts surface in my mind, but my Mark might have saved me from that fate. I may be fortunate enough to simply be killed like everyone else. A single blow and that is it. Gone from this Earth in the blink of an eye. Too fast to even feel it. Yes, that would be best.

The man in charge sighs. "What about the others?"

A Radical steps towards his leader. "The man has the Crescent, as does the woman. The young girl has the Cross."

"A Mediator?"

"Disgusting witches."

"Speaking to spirits? It's unnatural, I tell you!"

"I say hang 'em all!"

The Radicals talk among themselves as though we are not there, as though we are not human. Then again, in their eyes we aren't. We are lesser beings, unnatural, disgusting, and thus we deserve to die.

Dela's hair hangs in front of her face. It sticks around her jaw and forehead, held there by her tears. Her right sleeve is up to her elbow, revealing the Mark. Hers is a light blue, like glistening ice on the white of her skin. She meets my eyes and somehow, I manage a weak smile.

"Kill them all," Scar-face agrees. "Except this one." It takes me a moment to realize he is pointing at me. "We'll save her for later." My stomach churns.

"Please," I barely whisper. That one word, so insignificant and yet so powerful, drifts away on the wind.

Dela is staring intently over my shoulder, but when I turn, I see nothing. She comes back to herself with a shake of the head and her eyes wander to mine. She answers the question in my eyes with a terse nod and smiles.

Lightning-fast, the horses bustle into movement, as though spooked by a ghost. Caught by surprise, the Radicals fling themselves out of the way. I jump to the side, landing in the dirt. My elbows scrape against the earth and I rush to my feet. The man with the crooked teeth sees me and growls. He runs for me, hands outstretched.

"Elvira!" It is Dela calling. I see her standing on

the other side of the road with Mother and Father, and I cannot get my feet moving fast enough. I run to them and Mr. Crooked-Teeth gives chase. I hike up my skirts, holding them immodestly above my knees. Pulse racing, skin slick with sweat, breathing nearly impossible, I force myself into a sprint.

Mother clutches me in her arms when I reach them, but it is short-lived. A Radical reaches us, grabbing Father by the neck.

"Father!" I scream. His face turns a deep shade of blue, his fingers clawing at the hands clamped around his throat. I search the road, looking for anything I can use as a weapon. A large stick lies on the ground and I grab for it. Coming up behind the Radical, I raise the stick and swing. It hits against his head with a sickening thunk! I can hear his skull crack beneath my blow. Bile rises in my throat. He drops to the ground, blood matting his hair. My father falls to his knees, wheezing.

I stare at the ruby red as the sickening crack echoes in my mind again and again.

Hit—crack—collapse. Hit—crack—collapse.

The blood pools around my boots and I step back in shock.

"Elvira. Elvira!" My father's raspy voice filters through the endless song. *Smash. Crack! Thud.* "Elvira!"

Startled, I turn away from the hideous sight. My eyes dart from horror to horror. People run all around me. We are indeed at war, but war is not how I would describe this scene. Chaos. That is the word. Pure and utter chaos surrounds me in a whirlpool of cries and fire, bangs and explosions, blood and last breaths. My senses are on overload, and yet, silence is all I hear.

A cool hand wraps around my arm, pulling me down. I collapse to my knees, meeting the face of the Radical with the scar. I scream and he laughs a hideous laugh.

"No escapin' me, precious," he purrs and next thing I know, he is on top of me. My breath whooshes out of me as his fingers curl around my hair, plowing my face into the dirt. I cannot breathe! I inhale and choke, dirt filling my lungs.

Kicking and punching, I squirm beneath him. I pull at his hair, try to bite his hand, claw at his arms; anything to get him off! He flips me around so that I must gaze back into his monstrous face. His legs clasp tight around my thighs and he pins my arms against my ears. Like being submerged underwater, the muddled clamor quiets into a soft hum. I move my head from side to side as I struggle, the lurid din undulating like the feral surf.

"I want ta see those violet eyes as the life drains from 'em," he slurs.

That is when I see the glint of his dagger in the moonlight, raised just above my chest. I let out a strangled cry and squeeze my eyes shut, tensing for the pain. Unexpectedly, the weight releases and I am sure I have died when I hear Dela screaming in my ear.

"El, are you all right?"

I open my eyes and she is hovering over me, worry creasing her brow.

"Dela," I whisper in relief. She helps me up and we are off once again. I see Mother in Scar-face's clutches and I scream to her. A mottling of purples, blues, and blacks paints his cheek and a thin river of blood trickles down his forehead. I stare at Dela and she shrugs. The strength of my little sister has always surprised me, but I do wonder if perhaps, this time, she had some help from her... friends.

The Radical hears my scream and releases Mother, having found a new target. Me. Dela and I turn to run, but we are weighed down by our dresses and cannot catch our breath. Corsets were not made for running. He catches Dela's foot, dragging her back, and I slam my heel down on his hand. His yell fills the night, melding in perfect harmony with the chaos around us.

I help Dela to her feet and we run for the long grass just ahead. At the edge of the lengthy stalks, we look back. Fire paints the sky in an angry orange and black shadowy figures run amuck. I watch as a Radical lashes out with a knife and a man falls beneath the blow. I wince, turning away. I see Father, at last, caught in the grasp of a Radical. I begin to run forward, hoping to aid him, when I hear Mother call.

"No, Elvira!"

I turn and there she is. "We must help him!" I argue.

"No. You must flee. Take Dela. Run to the beach and don't turn back. Now, go! Go!" Her face shows her fear, but it shows something else, too. Something I cannot quite place.

"But, Mother, what about you and Father? We're not leaving you!"

"You'll do as I say. Now, run to the beach. Then, to the docks. There is a ship there—the RMS *Celtic*—leaving for America. You are to board it and not wait for your father and me. We will make sure you are not followed."

"But Mother—"

"Elvira," she warns.

"Those passenger ships are for refugees. We are forbidden!"

"You'll find a way. You always do," she says, too sweetly for the way I've talked to her. "Now, my dear Elvira, be brave for your sister and do as I say." Suddenly, I know what it is I could not place before. Hope. Hope that maybe Dela and I will escape. "We will meet again in New York."

A tear slides down my cheek and I nod. She bends down to Dela's level, placing a tender finger under her chin. "You be brave for your sister, too, now, you hear?"

She nods solemnly.

"I love you both dearly. Do be safe." She places a kiss on both our cheeks and pushes us towards the field. "Go on, now," she yells. "Go!"

Without a second glance, I turn and my feet are moving beneath me, Dela's hand gripped tightly in my own. We push through the long stalks. The swishing of our skirts against the grass and our heavy breathing drowns out the cries behind us. I stare mournfully at the white circle in the sky, its shadows and whorls guiding me towards the beach. I lock eyes with the man in the moon, my new friend, my only friend.

Everyone else is lost.

3
RETURNING

The porcelain face with the hollow eyes and lips as red as blood crunches beneath my foot. Only half a pale face, half a demure smile, half a rosy cheek. The rest of the cracked pieces lie scattered among the ashes. In Dela's hand, the fabric of the doll's dress, torn and tattered.

Everything so unbelievably torn and tattered. All destroyed. This was a bad idea. This was a very, very bad idea. Why return to the ghosts of your memories?

Soot and ash fall from the sky like an angel's wing feathers. Cast from heaven, they rain down upon those still living, upon us. Their gray bodies cling to the grass blades like dew. I can almost pretend that the feathery ashes resting upon Dela's golden strands are snowflakes. Except, rather than reflect the light like snow, the ashes engulf it, darkening the world as well as my mood.

I stand rooted where I am, unable to go any further outside the grass stalks we escaped through the previous night. Fear of what I might find beneath the ashes swallows me the same way they swallow light. Dela runs ahead. I follow her with my eyes.

The images of her running through these streets the previous summer—her feet bare, her hair loose, my fuming mother close behind—plays side-by-side with the present scene. How drastically that scene has changed. From sprouting flowers, hot cobblestone streets, and cloudless skies to nothing but endless gray. The inequity of it all makes my throat throb and my eyes swim. We knew it was only a matter of time. We knew they would come. But knowing never seems to make it any less sudden.

"El!" Dela's voice filters through the wall of dust. Her small form has grown much farther away and I can barely make it out through the filmy air. "El! Come quick!"

Terror drills into my skull, making my teeth vibrate. What did she find? Surely not a body. Please, not anyone we know. Please, let it be a stranger. I instantly regret having thought it. Only a terrible, monstrous person would not think a stranger's life is just as important... and yet, that same thought continues to ring in my ears. Not even the guilt can drown it out.

I race towards her voice, my boots leaving footprints in the ash behind me. Slowly, her form becomes more distinct until I am right beside her, panting with fear and exhaustion. Dela looks to me. Tears well in her eyes and I see the sympathy floundering in the crystal droplets.

With a hiccupping gasp, I realize where we are standing. If it were last afternoon, I would be standing next to my butterfly bush, but the miniature purple flowers of yesterday have dissipated into nothingness. A charred skeleton of lifeless branches is the only sign it ever existed. Beneath my feet would have been my white rock-roses. They had just started blooming, their little white buds just beginning to form, but the fire destroyed them before they were given the chance to blossom. The fire destroyed everything.

I move through the blackened land that was once my thriving garden. The scorched leaves crackle like fire under the weight of my footsteps. I feel Dela follow me, but neither of us speaks. Our silence says it all. There are no words to describe how I feel. The utter loss is like a nail driven into my chest—piercing my heart and exiting out through my back. I see the nail inside me and yet cannot believe it. Too numb to comprehend.

Dela stands just behind me, and I hear her muttering to herself. I catch the words "ashes to ashes" and reach behind me. Somehow my hand finds hers, pulling her towards me. With our arms wrapped around one another, we peer up at the very sight I had been avoiding.

Before us lie the remains of the only home I have ever known. The roof has caved in under the heat, the top floor buckled and collapsed like a wooden avalanche of broken memories. Only the front entry wall still stands. Torn from one of its hinges, the front door hangs open in defeat. The fire's trail coats the wood in black, only the top of the door remotely resembling what once was. The glass window has exploded just like that of my bedroom. A few broken pieces still cling to the frame, refusing to yield. I can see the glass dust glittering upon the ground, and almost find it beautiful in a strange way.

"We should go." Dela speaks so quietly that I am not sure I heard her until she opens her mouth a second time. "We did not come back to mourn over what once was and what will never be again."

Her words are like a slap in the face. And although I know she is only trying to cope, a tiny flicker of anger ignites inside me. I am not yet ready to admit my whole world is changing. To accept that I will never live in this destroyed home again, that I will never again tend to this once beautiful garden, is simply too much to undertake in one day.

Pursing my lips, I nod my head in agreement nonetheless. Without a word, Dela retreats from the devastation. As though peering through another person's eyes, I take one more look at the fire's sorrowing success before following my sister out of the backyard and the burnt remnants of my garden.

I stand in the middle of the room, afraid to touch anything. I can hear Dela rummaging in the chest to my left. She is not at all shy about going through another's things, and her lack of decorum worries me. I instantly chide myself. I am beginning to sound just like my marriage-obsessed mother.

"A woman's sole purpose is to find a husband, not to whittle away her time soiling her gloves in a garden!" she often told me.

But my gardening was never any competition with Dela's adventurousness. "You will never marry if you do not learn some propriety, Dela Marie Hamilton!" Mother would scream at Dela's back as she ran out the door towards the ocean, her dress slinging through the mud as she went. I smile at the memory.

"Ew! Look here, El. It's a pair of Daniel Thompson's knickers!" I turn my head just in time to see Dela's face contort into a form of playful disgust. She tosses them at me and I shriek. By now, we are both giggling uncontrollably, the pent up anguish of the recent events finding a short release. "I do hope this was not Daniel's only pair," Dela jokes, but the past tense of the statement makes our momentary joy instantly dissipate.

We thought maybe the Thompsons had escaped since their house is tucked back in the woods on the very edge of town, but there is no way to know for sure. Unsettled, I lean back against the small bed as Dela finds the clothes we need. We agreed that we would be less conspicuous as boys. Being Marked is bad enough, but being girls only worsens our predicament.

"All right," she says, attempting to stand with her arms full of clothing. "I think I have the essentials. Should we check the kitchen one last time?"

I shake my head. "There is no use. If there was food, we would have found it already. Besides, we don't want to miss the ship. It will be a long walk."

Dela's lips pucker in disappointment. "I suppose you are right."

I smile sadly at her, wishing I could give another answer. Relieving her of the clothes, I walk out of the room and down the steps into the parlor. I give the room one more brief inspection, making sure everything is in its place. I nearly laugh aloud at the absurdity of it. The last thing the Thompsons will worry about is two girls breaking into their house and stealing a few articles of clothing. They are Marked, and just like us, they have much bigger problems than theft.

Besides, if they ever do return, they will be returning to a ghost town. Only one other person was left breathing, and she is standing right next to me. Everyone else is either gone or dead. The only building free from harm is the one we currently stand in. All others have been reduced to ash and rubble. The Radicals destroyed my beautiful little village and everyone inside it, and then simply walked away. I know because I watched them do it. I watched them take the dead's carriages and flee the scene of their crimes. Knowing for sure they had all fled is the only reason I agreed to return.

The anger and pain hits me like a sudden upsurge. Dela lays a warm hand against my arm, a reassuring touch. I close my eyes and take a deep breath. Forget it all for now, I tell myself. Let the images from last night and today vanish—at least until we make it onto the ship.

With this new goal in mind, I walk out of the house and within ten steps I am standing in the ashy silt once again. Focused on keeping my promise to my mother, I do not think about the ash's origins—about the people, buildings, and memories that create the silky deposit.

No, instead, I am walking through snow. The pieces of debris floating through the air are flower petals caught on the breeze. And everyone is just playing hide-and-go-seek; we, of course, are the seekers. Yes, everything is not as bad as it seems.

At least, that's what I pretend.

4
SNEAKING

The horn's dismal cry cuts through the crowd and my head snaps up.

"Dela, do hurry!" I yell.

"I'm almost done," she grumbles. "There." She steps out from behind the bin and smiles. "How do I look? Is it better?"

"You look like a boy," I say matter-of-factly. "And yes, the string helps," I lie, referring to the thread she has turned into a makeshift belt. Considering she almost lost her pants multiple times during the walk to the docks, the string seemed like a quick fix, but in truth it does little for her hopeless cause.

"Perfect." She shoots me a girlish grin and steps by me. Her trouser hems drag on the ground, and she tries desperately to hold them up. It is a shame we hadn't found knickerbockers. They would have been a much better fit, I think.

Unfortunately, Daniel Thompson was about two times

the size of my dainty sister. The blazer is far too long, but it serves its purpose. I tighten my tie and lower my bowler hat. I pat my chest, wondering if it is evident I am not a man.

I follow Dela out onto the cobblestone street, leaving our dresses in the alley. We will not need them where we are going. Makeshift shops rise up on either side of us. Colorful fabrics and glittering jewelry cascade over the sides of some fronts, creating a waterfall of glorious teals and fuchsias, emeralds and silvers. The sweet scent of fresh baked goods mixes with the salt-filled air. Hawkers stand outside. Their commanding voices permeate the small space as they try desperately to make a sale.

"Bread, my dear boy... to bring home to your family, perhaps?" a woman says to Dela, a loaf of bread outstretched in her grimy hands. My sister shakes her head, but sneaks me a grin, for our charade is working.

"Care for some flowers, lad? A good looking man such as yourself must have a lady, eh?" a man with a bushy mustache says to me. Lovely. I'm a handsome boy, but an awkward girl. Funny how things work out. I straighten my tie and shake my head.

"No, thank you," I say, my voice too high. It has given me away for sure. Dela shoots me a look. "I mean... No, thank you, sir," I try again, taking on a deep and gravelly tone. The man nods, turning away.

A tiny smirk pricks at my lips in triumph before I

hear him whisper to his wife, "No wonder he hasn't got a lady. Poor lad hasn't even hit puberty yet." His wife clucks her tongue in sympathy. A blush warms my cheeks and raises red splotches along the back of my neck. Hurriedly, I catch up to Dela.

The horn lets out its mournful call once again and we make haste, nearly being trampled by a carriage on our way to the pier. The bitter smell of the sea makes my nose wrinkle, and I lust for the sweet smell of the lilacs in my garden. They always bloomed so beautifully this time of year. I picture their stems burned to crisps, and a chill passes through me. I shall miss that garden.

"Elvira, what shall we do?" Dela pulls at my sleeve and I stare down at her girly-boy face peeking out from beneath her homburg. Its wide brim conceals her crystal blue eyes.

Looking before me, I gasp at the sheer size of the RMS *Celtic* resting on the water. It is a monstrosity. Passengers stand on the three decks, waving to their families and friends below. Over six temporary walkways lead up to the ship from the dock. People bustle around us, moving up the walks onto the ship as workers take their bags. A woman walks by me wearing lavish pearls and a long purple dress with a pigeon breast. The latest style. I stare dolefully at my oversized sacker coat and matching waistcoat. As much as I hate dresses, I must admit they are much more flattering. I pull at the stiff collar resting just beneath my jaw.

Distracted by the sight of a car being lifted by a crane, I dismiss my itching neck. The vehicle's black coat shines in the sunlight. A steering wheel sticks out up to the seat, exposed to the open air.

"El, how are we to get on the ship?"

"Do you ever think we'd be able to own a car?" I say wistfully.

Dela rolls her eyes. "No. Such luxuries belong to the rich and the rich alone. Besides, I prefer horses." She places her hands on her hips in a girly manner. "Do you have a plan or not?"

"Do remember you're a boy," I say. "And yes, as a matter of fact, I do have a plan." I reach for her hand, pulling her towards the back end of the ship. Many workers go up and down the ramp, holding large and small crates alike.

"You must be joking," Dela says, wrenching her hand out of my own. "You're not serious!"

Unfortunately, I am all too serious. The plan stinks almost as much as the pile of horse manure we passed in the street, but terrible or not—

"Well, unless you have a better plan to sneak onto the ship..." She does not answer. "No? Then I suppose we are stuck with mine. Now, come along. Quickly, while no one is looking."

I glance around, watching as the last man walks up the plank. I open the nearest crate, ducking a heavy bronze Tiffany lamp into the ocean. The delicately painted flowers upon its base almost seem to wither as it hits the water. Scanning the area for the workers, I decide the coast is clear and help my sister inside. She glowers up at me, and I shut the lid before that glare destroys my impulsive determination.

"Don't make a noise until I give you the signal," I whisper.

"What's the signal?"

"I'll... whistle." Moving unto the next box, I heave a large vase over the side of the pier and close myself inside. *Please let the workmen pick us up.* A second later, the crate jostles and I bite my lip to restrain my yelp when my head bangs against the side.

"Och, this box is heavier than I remember," he says.

Excuse me?

"Too heavy for you, eh?" another worker laughs.

"Too heavy!" he scoffs, hitching the box higher to prove himself. I bite down harder to keep from squealing and the copper taste of blood mixes in my mouth. Men and their ridiculous obsession with proving their superiority. I resist the urge to spit.

The man could not have been less gentle. My box is set down gruffly and I listen to his retreating steps. I wait for what seems to be forever. Crate after crate is carried in and set down beside mine.

"I think that's the last of 'em," I hear someone say,

and my heart leaps for joy. My legs are cramped and my backside has already fallen asleep. I think of the scolding I would receive from Mother if ever I voiced this thought and instantly shut her memory out of my mind.

The sound of metal on metal echoes around the room and through the thin wood of the crate. Was that the cargo room door closing? Are the men all gone? A final cry sounds from the horn, a farewell to those still standing on the docks. The ship lurches before picking up a gentle lolling. We are moving at last! My heart constricts in triumph. Finally, at sea! I have succeeded and we shall reach America and meet with my parents and all shall be right.

I was naïve to think it.

I whistle.

5
HIDING

"I'm going to be sick."

I turn my head to gaze at Dela. A sheen of sweat glistens on her abnormally pale face. I search the space around me and spot a small bucket. Reaching out my foot, I nudge it with my toe, sending it rolling towards her side of the room. It slides to a stop by her calf and she groans.

"There is no way I am going to vomit into that thing," she says stubbornly.

I shrug. "It's either that or your shirt. Your choice."

She shoots a half-hearted glare in my direction before pulling the bucket unto her lap. A second later the sounds of her gagging echo around the small space. I find myself growing sick at the sound of her retching, and I grimace.

"Are you quite done?" I ask, irritation creeping into my voice.

She scowls, wiping her sleeve across her mouth. "Terribly sorry. Next time I'll tell my stomach to consider my dear sister before deciding to heave its contents up my throat!"

"Keep your voice down," I scold, ignoring her comment.

A bang, like a gunshot. A sound I have become all too familiar with reaches us from somewhere far overhead. The muffled echo rings in my ears and I look to Dela, who shakes her head, refusing to acknowledge the bang as anything more than a noise. A splash follows quickly thereafter, but we disregard it. With new vigor, Dela continues her complaining.

I lean against a crate, my arms folded across my chest and my ankles crossed. Closing my eyes, I shut out Dela's insistent moans and concentrate on the sloshing of the sea against the ship.

"I loathe boats. There is a reason people were not given fins. We're simply not meant for the water," my sister mutters to herself before bending over the bucket a second time. "Horrid taste."

"Horrid smell," I say, putting a hand to my nose.

We exchange a quick glance; our weak laughter bounces off the mounds of crates and back into our ears. It sounds foreign, strained and forced. We let it die, allowing our short burst of mirth to pass in a few weak giggles before it floats away into silence.

"How much longer will we be on this dreadful ship?" A trace of worry hides behind the whining. I look at her thoughtfully, trying to figure out how she is taking all of this, when she drops her head into the bucket a third time.

I shrug. "I overheard the workers saying it would be about a week."

Dela stands shakily and begins to pace. She wobbles a few times, her legs not yet accustomed to the movement of the sea. "Kill me now," she mumbles.

An awkward silence permeates the space between us, her comment filling our minds with images of the previous night, of our parents, of home. I stifle the memories and go back to concentrating on the water's steady sloshing.

"Elvira," she whispers. "I'm hungry."

Food! The simplest of things, and I forgot!

"Tomorrow, Dela. I shall get us food tomorrow. Sleep for now," I say, much calmer than I feel.

She sighs before rolling over on her side and curling into a ball. When her heavy breathing at last permeates the room, I allow my pent up emotions to finally spill over in an onslaught of silent sobs. I cry for my parents, for my garden, for my sister... for myself. I cry because I am hungry and do not know how I will feed us come tomorrow. I cry because there is nothing more for me to do.

A laugh filters through my sobs. At first, I think I have finally reached hysterics, but a sharper, deeper laugh mixes with the other and I am sure it is not me. I stiffen, every hair on my body standing at attention. Two or more men are laughing outside the cargo room, only a few feet away from where I lie. My gaze fixates on the door.

"Did you hear about the vermin that tried to sneak onto the ship?"

A weight settles on my heart. Certainly they do not mean us! How could they possibly know? I place a hand against the nearest crate, steadying myself as dizzying fear swells up through my chest. Light filters through the bottom of the door, the men's black shadows dancing across its length.

"Surely, you don't mean..."

"Aye. That's exactly what I mean. One of them tried to pass as one of us, tried to sneak into third class."

The idea of attempting such a feat and being caught... it is simply too much. Even worse? The idea that with the simple opening of a door, we could be next.

"Chap didn't realize the attendants check every passenger's arms before boarding?"

"Suppose not, considering he's floating face down in the ocean by now." The man chuckles.

The other gasps and the first man continues his story merrily, happy for the attention.

"Aye, the attendant gave him a good beating before he shot him right in front of the crowd. I swear his blood ran black as death and oh, how the crowd gaped and cheered! The attendants threw the body overboard for the sharks." He laughs, and then adds, "Though not even the sharks would bother with the vile lad!"

The men join in rambunctious guffawing. The bang

from earlier surfaces in my mind and I shiver. An image of Dela and I floating face down in the water, sharks circling us in fluid movements, runs through my thoughts. I cringe at the notion and force it out of my head. And they call us disgusting, evil, violent...

Fear gives way to anger. It surges through my veins. I have to force myself to stay seated to keep from ripping open the door and... and... I don't know what. After all, I am powerless. I pull my sleeve up and am mesmerized by the Mark. It burns a bright violet, seeming to glow in the dark of the room. I trace a finger around the endless circle and the intricate cross in the middle.

"Why me?" I whisper. Why must I be the one cursed with the Mark that does not work? Why must I have the Mark no one else has seen before? There is talk of it. Oh, yes, people have heard of it. An old folktale that says the one with the Circle and Cross has great power, but folktales are fiction—fairy tales. Not real.

And the idea that I may be one of the Lost—those Marked without powers—continues to seem more and more likely. But to be one is to be a disgrace to your family. My parents insist that I am simply a late bloomer, but most Marked show some sign of their powers by the age of six. I should have known my powers over ten years ago! Should have, but didn't. The word Lost has haunted me these past few years almost as much as Radicals.

"We best be going back. The men are gathering for

cigars soon," one man says.

"Ah, yes, indeed."

Their retreating footsteps grow faint and I breathe a sigh of relief. We are safe. For now. Leaning my head back, I close my eyes and allow the gentle lolling of the boat to erase my thoughts and eventually, rock me to sleep.

6
STEALING

I lie on my back, staring at the wooden planks that form a low ceiling. Holes and whorls dot the lumber, and I connect them, turning mishap marks into war heroes and horses, puppies and flowers. I think back to lying in my garden beneath the midnight blue sky. The smell of roses and lavender would lull me into a sweet stupor as I traced the constellations with my mind. Sometimes Father joined me.

He would come out of the house in his dark trousers and loosened tie simply to lie beside his eldest daughter. And I would watch him as he traced lines with his fingers in the air, creating stories to match the images so vividly outlined in the sky.

"Your garden is as beautiful as ever," he would say. "Like your flowers, you have blossomed into a proper young lady."

His words would make me smile and we would return our attention to the stars, feeling warmth in the knowledge that we were not alone.

I turn my head, wishing the crate lying beside me was my Father, wishing it could wrap me in its arms and tell me everything will be okay. I wait for it to speak. I wait to hear its heartbeat. I wait to feel something besides the dull ache of grief at the pit of my stomach.

I wait for things that will never come.

Dela sleeps at the opposite side of the room, but we are miles apart. I lie in her company and feel more alone than ever before.

A sharp pang of hunger joins the aching and I grudgingly sit upright.

"No time for pity, El," I tell myself as I tighten my tie and replace my bowler hat atop my head. I consider waking Dela to tell her I am leaving, but think better of it as I remember her groggy tendencies. Tiptoeing towards the door, I crack it open an inch and peek outside. An empty corridor leads to a stairwell. I slip through the opening. The security of the cargo room calls out to me, a persuading cry I yearn to obey, as I step closer and closer to the very people who want me dead.

—

Assaulted.
Assaulted by sights. Assaulted by smells. Assaulted by noises.

The cargo room had been a bubble. A bubble of calm protecting us from the world just above. The atmosphere had been stale and dry, but on the top deck, the wind whips around my face and I struggle to keep my hair concealed below my hat. It carries with it the spray of the sea. I inhale deeply, soaking up the fresh, moist air.

The murmurs of many people float across the air, snippets of words and conversations. A group of women to my right gazes at the horizon, their faces raised to the heavens. I imagine puppet strings attached to their noses and must suppress a snicker. By the sight of the pearls dripping from their necks and ears, I assume they are first-class passengers.

A young girl stands on the lowest rung of the rail, bending over to see the waves break against the ship. Her father stands just behind her, his hands on her waist to keep her from falling over. She wears a white dress, the hems frayed and torn. Most definitely third-class. One of the women from first-class gazes over at the two and whispers to her friends. They break into giggles before raising their noses even higher and walking away.

I wonder how they would react to someone like me, someone who is below the lowest, below even those in steerage.

Annoyed by their superior attitudes, I turn away, scanning the deck for a sign of food. Through a wall of windows, I see the dining room. Girls wearing wide-brimmed hats and lingerie dresses sit around a table drinking tea and laughing behind their crisp, white napkins. Men in black morning coats and trousers talk business, their bushy mustaches moving up and down as they speak. I grow jealous of their leisurely lifestyle, wanting to knock the teacups from their hands. Thinking of Dela, I resist the urge and surreptitiously step through the entrance.

White tablecloths adorn the tables, polished silverware and crystal glasses set at each place. Elegantly folded napkins rest before every seat atop cream plates. Croissants and pastries on tiered platters inhabit every occupied table, but there is no chance of inconspicuously stealing a few. My stomach rumbles. My mouth waters. The heavenly smells of the kitchen waft through the air.

I stand in the corner, ogling the food with eager eyes.

"Excuse me, sir," a waiter says as he steps by me. In his hands is a large platter full of cranberry bread and French toast, muffins and rolls. The aroma is torturous.

"Mr. Simmons," someone calls from the kitchen, "you have forgotten the tea!"

The man called Simmons sits the tray on a nearby table with an agitated sigh and walks back into the kitchen. It rests only a few steps away, food ready for the taking. I eye the kitchen door one last time and pounce upon the table. Quickly, I begin filling my pockets, an advantageous addition to my trousers. Dress-makers never did seem to understand the value of pockets.

"What do you think you are doing?"

My head snaps up. The waiter is back.

His face is red. His eyes narrowed, staring right at me. They flicker down to my bulging pockets and I freeze. A white teapot with rose blossoms painted on the front threatens to crack under the pressure of his white-knuckled hands. Without thinking, I turn and run.

"Hey!" he yells after me. "Stop!"

I do not listen. The wind rushes past my ears, the pants giving me a new freedom as I run. My heart is pounding, my lungs sucking in salty air. I glance over my shoulder; the waiter is pushing through the tables after me, apologizing to each passenger he bumps into along the way.

At last, I make it to the entrance. I can feel the diners' eyes on my back, but I do not stop. My legs carry me across the deck, sidestepping each obstacle thrust in my way with ease. The man's yells cannot make it through the haze enveloping my thoughts. Running is the purest ecstasy, the purest freedom; it creates a fog that eliminates the surrounding world. I take another glance behind me and smile at how far behind the waiter has become. He shall never catch me, I think joyfully, before... Smack!

The hard hit knocks me to the ground, and I lie sprawled across the deck on my back. My breath whooshes from my lungs and the world floods back in. I lift my gaze to see what hard object I had run into and gasp. The shadowy shape of a man looms over me, but I cannot see his face, blinded by the glaring sun behind him.

My hat lies upside down beside me, my hair falling down across my shoulders. Fear beats through my veins. My second biggest secret whips around my face in the form of black ringlets.

"Stop right there!"

The towering man's head snaps up and I crane my neck to see, too. The waiter! He runs forward, still meters away but drawing closer every second. I gaze at the young man and then at the waiter. What am I to do? Snapping my hat up, I stand, rearing to run, when the man grabs my arm. I gasp, looking down at my pale arm in his strong grip. I pull against him, but his firm hold does not waver.

Confused and frightened, I meet his gaze. He stares back at me, his abnormally light green eyes cold and calculating. His skin is tan, a few freckles dotting his nose. Long lashes frame his startling eyes and his pink lips press into a thin line. His deep brown hair falls over his forehead, disheveled. I find myself realizing he is handsome, beautiful even, and perhaps only a year older than me. Eighteen at the very most.

"Put your hat back on," he says, his voice deeper than I expected. I peer over his shoulder and see the waiter coming towards us. With difficulty, I secure my hair beneath the bowler. Just as I tuck away the last curl, the man jogs over to us, placing his hands on his knees as he takes deep breaths. It is clearly not every day that he must chase a thieving girl-boy.

"Terribly sorry, Mr. Laurence, sir," he says, and straightens. I find it strange that the waiter should know his name. This Mr. Laurence must be a first-class passenger, and a very important one at that. "If you would be so kind as to hand over the lad, I'll let you continue on your way."

The young man holding my arm smirks. "I think not."

I must not be the only one surprised by this turn of events, for the waiter is staring at the young man, dumbfounded. I stare, too, unsure as to what he is doing. Or more importantly, why?

"Here's what you are going to do," the young man says, a clear tone of authority lacing his voice. "You are going to return to the kitchen and inform anyone who asks that you were mistaken. You will not mention this occurrence to anyone. You will return to your life as though the past five minutes never occurred." He digs in his pockets and puts a handful of shillings in the waiter's hands. "Do we have an understanding?"

"But—Sir—" the waiter stammers. I almost feel sorry for him.

Holding up a hand, the young man silences him. "No questions. Do as I say and be gone."

The waiter nods his head in a short bow and leaves,

sneaking incredulous glances over his shoulder.

Still holding my arm, the young man turns, pulling me along with him. I follow behind, afraid to speak if he should change his mind about saving me. He marches me through doors and corridors, through an airy tea room, and what I am sure is the ballroom, until we stop before a door on the third level. He pulls a key from his blazer pocket and opens the door, stepping inside and pulling me in after him.

The cabin is large with a small living room branching into a dining room and two bedrooms. I catch a glimpse of a claw foot bathtub through a door to my right. Whoever this young man is, he has money and lots of it. He swings me around onto a pink chaise and closes the door, leaning against it purposefully.

Out of the corner of my eye, I see a maid scurry into the closest room, afraid she has stumbled upon an intimate moment between her master and his new lady friend. I find myself wondering if she must do this often when he brings guests.

"Who are you?" The sudden sound of his deep voice jars me out of my reverie. His tone skips over all pleasantries, and I grope for a reply.

"I beg your pardon?"

He moves forward, bending down until his nose is only inches away from mine. "Who—are—you?"

I shake my head. "I—I don't—"

He sighs, rubbing his light eyes before setting them back on me. A touch of humor glistens in the green of his irises. "Let's start with your name, Mr.—" He pauses, then laughs. "Or should I say, Miss... ?"

"Hamilton. Miss Elvira Hamilton," I answer squeakily. It is only after the words have left my mouth that I realize I should have given him a false name. Mistake number one.

"Elvira," he muses, testing the sound of it on his own tongue. "Very well, Vi. My name is Adam Laurence."

I scowl, deciding I do not like this Mr. Laurence, no matter what he has done for me. He exudes the attitude of a pompous, rich heir; his use of my first name is inexcusably rude.

"Well, Mr. Laurence—"

"Adam," he corrects.

My eyes narrow even further as I stand, returning to my full height, still inches shorter than his. "Mr. Laurence," I say, putting as much malice and indignation in his name as possible, "thank you for going out of your way to help me. I am much obliged to you; however, I really must be going. Good day." I move towards the door, but he gets there faster, leaning back against it to keep me from leaving.

His booming laugh startles me and I stare at him, not amused.

"You honestly believed I would let you leave? You're a criminal!"

"Am not!" I yell childishly. He gazes down at my overflowing pockets and raises his brows. "You do not know me, Mr. Laurence. Please do not pretend otherwise."

"Ah, but I will know you."

I throw my hands in the air, forgetting all manners. "This is positively absurd. I am leaving."

He ignores me, but grabs the wrist of my outstretched hand before I so much as touch the doorknob. I see violet peeking out from beneath his fingers and suck in a gulp of air through my teeth. "I will know you just as soon as you answer my questions."

I pause, wrenching my hand out of his grasp. Furtively, I pull my sleeve back down to cover the Mark.

"You cannot possibly know someone by asking a few questions; not truly, anyhow." I sigh. "If I answer your questions, will you allow me to leave?"

Raising a hand to his chest, he crosses his heart with two smooth strokes of a finger. "I promise."

"Go on, then. Ask your questions," I say, and quickly add, "but you only get three."

"Three questions! You are far more infuriating and stubborn than I would have initially believed, but three shall do." He taps his index finger against his chin as he paces before the door. "All right, question number one." He pauses, a devilish smirk sidling up his face. "Do you find me exceptionally attractive or only moderately so?" He winks and bares his teeth in a flashy grin. My mouth drops open and my violet eyes widen in shock. How can anyone be so exasperatingly audacious?

He chuckles at my reaction, as if I and everyone else in the world exist purely for his own amusement. "Calm down, Vi. It was only a joke. The real question number one: Why is a pretty girl such as yourself disguised as a boy and resorting to minor criminal offenses like stealing baked goods?"

My thoughts catch on the word pretty, but I instantly dismiss it. "That's two questions and your initial question counts, as well."

"You didn't even answer! Although, I suppose your eyes did say it all." He grins smugly.

I glare at his smile, wanting to swipe it from his face. "My eyes said nothing. You didn't get an answer because you do not deserve an answer."

He smirks. "Very well. I still want the answers to the last two then." He steps forward and his dark brown hair gleams in the light cast by a Tiffany lamp much like the one I dumped into the ocean. Those green eyes find mine and I relinquish with a sigh.

"Clearly, I disguise myself because I do not want people knowing I am a woman. As for the pastries, I was hungry."

"Those are obvious answers." He takes a step closer, raising his chin and crossing his arms.

"They were obvious questions." I mimic his movement,

my nose only inches away from his puffed out chest.

"But why do you not want people knowing you are a woman?" he asks.

I shake my head, two black curls falling down around my shoulders from beneath the bowler hat. "You had your three questions, Mr. Laurence; now you must let me pass."

Reluctantly, he steps aside, but keeps a hand on the doorknob. "Fair enough, but first, tell me what cabin you are staying in."

I smile. He still believes I am a passenger on the ship. If only he knew.

"Trust me. You would not be able to find me even if I told you," I say, suppressing a smirk. "Goodbye, Mr. Laurence." He opens the door for me and I step outside, securing my hair back beneath the hat as I walk.

I feel those strange green eyes burning into my back as I amble down the hall and turn my head—he's standing just outside his door.

He waves. "Until next time, Vi!"

There will be no next time. The minute I return to the cargo room, I will be stuck there until the *Celtic* docks in New York. The aggravating man and I will never meet again. He will return to his lavish balls and will marry a girl whose parents look to have a wealthy son-in-law. I will meet with my parents in New York and we will go into hiding until the war has ended.

Two separate worlds that will never, ever collide.

———

7
LYING

When I return, Dela is awake.

"Where were you? I was positive you had been caught and fed to a giant squid!"

"Ah, to be twelve again. Such imagination," I say. She scowls and I smile. "Honestly, Dela, you mustn't allow yourself to get so worked up over nonsense."

Her brow knits together in annoyance. "At least I have an excuse for my imagination. What about yours? Lying out in that garden of yours all night making up stories based on make-believe pictures in the sky!"

I feel my face grow heated. This is silly, I tell myself, but then why am I so angry?

"They are called constellations! You're being childish!"

"Says the sixteen-year-old to the twelve-year-old. I am a child! What's your excuse?"

I step back, wanting to hit something, to scream at the top of my lungs! "Stop doing that!" I yell.

"What?"

"Turning everything back on me!" Spinning around on my heel, I stomp over to the opposite corner and sit down on a small crate, my back facing Dela. I pull a croissant from my pocket and begin tearing it apart with my teeth in a most unladylike fashion.

As I eat, I hear Dela sniff at the air once, twice, three times. "What is that glorious smell?" She turns in a full circle before her icy blue stare finally settles on me. "You brazen dingbat! You had food all this time! The nerve of you!" She stomps up behind me and I swivel into a standing position. Her mouth gapes open in astonishment. "You must give me some, El!"

"I mustn't do anything."

"El!" She shrieks in exasperation and makes for the croissant in my hand. I dodge her, holding it above my head.

"You don't deserve any!"

She jumps up, swinging her arms wildly, but I hold it just out of reach.

"You're impossible!" she yells. "Just give me a piece! I am starving!"

Just as I am about to retort, a loud bang echoes outside the cargo room, followed by a mix of deep voices. We both look to the door and back at each other. Dela's eyes widen with fear, a mirror image of my own.

"Now you've done it," I hiss.

"Me? What about you?"

"Would you stop doing that?"

"Doing what?"

"That!" I whisper-yell. "Stop it!"

The voices grow louder as they come closer, and we freeze. Just like before, a small group of men stands just beyond the door. Panic swarms through my brain like a horde of wasps. They buzz against my skull, hampering my ability to think straight. A closed door can only do so much. Last time, we were lucky. It stayed closed. Our secrets remained safe. This time, however, I fear our luck may change.

"Are you sure—?" a voice starts, but is hastily interrupted.

"I am telling you, sir. It sounded like screaming. An argument, maybe."

"All right. Thank you, gentlemen. Please, return to your chess game and I'll have a look-see."

Retreating footsteps overpower the one pair of footsteps looming closer to the door—to us. I push Dela back behind a crate and make to hide myself. A fan of light widens across the floor as the door is pushed open. It casts over my shoe, and then my pant-leg, and before I know it my entire body is glowing with the light from the hall. I become rigid. There is no chance for me now. I turn towards the door.

"Hello? Who is there?" the man calls. On cue, I collapse to my knees and break out in sobs.

The man shuffles over to my side and bends down to my level.

"Are you all right, lad? What are you doing in here?"

I shake my head, making sure not to move so much that my hair might fall down. "I have just proposed to the love of my life," I tell him in a deep voice, keeping my face buried in my hands, "but her parents will not allow it."

I take a peek at the man. His forehead is creased with concern, even his mustache seeming to frown in sympathy. "Dear me," he sighs.

"I just wanted a place to be alone. I am terribly sorry to have inconvenienced you," I whisper, wiping at my nose.

The man helps me to my feet, and I thank him. "Is there anyone I can take you back to?"

I pause. I had not foreseen this fault in my plan. Who can you take me to? How about my father? My mother? Can you take me to them? You would all get along so well. Them with their Marks and you with your hateful, ignorant nature. No? What a shame.

"Mr. Adam Laurence," I say. What are you doing, El? Without thinking, the name had popped out, now hanging there, out in the open. "He is a good friend."

"Very well. Mr. Laurence is a good man."

I can only nod in response as he leads me through the door. A glance over my shoulder reveals Dela's bright blue eyes, glowing in the blackness. They ask me a million questions I can only answer with a careful expression, telling her to sit tight, that I will be back. I make sure to drop the rolls from my pockets on my way out. At least now I know she is fed, I think, before stepping out into the hall, following behind the gentleman who thinks I am a boy, who thinks I am a passenger, who thinks I am like him.

What an ignorant fool.

—

The man makes pleasantries as we walk. I do not make a sound, simply nod and smile. Every few minutes, I wipe at a forced tear or sniffle. If we were not in the midst of a war, and it wasn't so tremendously frowned upon by my mother, I would make a splendid actress. He continues the one-sided conversation, telling me I seem like a fine man and that he cannot fathom why anyone would not want me as a son-in-law.

Maybe it is because I am not a boy, I think. Or it may have something to do with the violet Mark on my left wrist. Oh, wait, I know! It is because my nonexistent powers frighten them! Yes, that must be why my fictitious parents-in-law-to-be will not consent my elopement with their imaginary daughter!

Stupid, ignorant fool! His lack of knowledge irks me. He should know that I had to leave my mother and father behind. He should know that I have no way of feeding the only family I have left, and that I finally deserve the title of "criminal" so casually thrown around by the Radicals. He should know that I am hated for the powers I do not possess. He should know that I am a girl. He should know all of these things! But they are my burden and mine alone. The price of secrets.

"I am sure the girl's parents will find reason within time. You merely must be patient," he continues.

"Yes," I say. "I will do just that."

He smiles, teeth and lips jutting out from beneath that bushy mass. "There's a good lad!" He pats me on the back; I stare at him accusingly before realizing he has done nothing wrong. I am, after all, a boy. A strong, brave boy who can easily handle a firm pat on the back. Right?

We turn into Mr. Laurence's hall and the seed of fear implanted in my chest begins to blossom. What if he chooses not to help me again? After the way I treated him, I would not be surprised.

"Well, here we are," the man states, pausing before the door. He raps his knuckles against the wood finishing.

The moment of truth. Suddenly, the door swings inwards. A man appears in the doorway. I strain my neck to look at him: thin mustache, chiseled chin—everything you'd expect in a footman. Towering over the man and me by a good ten inches or so, the footman wears the proper white tie and tails with brass buttons stamped with the family crest. He greets us with minimal words and turns from the door, looking at someone hidden from our view.

"Call for Mr. Laurence, sir," he says. His voice is husky, laced with boredom and deference. "Just a moment," a man's voice replies from inside the room, and the empty doorway is suddenly occupied by the smooth countenance of Mr. Laurence as his footman steps to the side. He looks to me with a smile. If he is surprised to see me, he does not show it.

Looking back to the servant, he says, "Thank you, John. You may return to your duties."

With a short bow, the footman departs. Mr. Laurence watches him as he goes, as though waiting for him to falter, before returning that mischievous smile of his to me.

"How may I help you?"

The man puts a hand behind my back, pushing me forward. I gasp, having forgotten he was there. "Found this lad here in the cargo room. He claims he knows you."

"Ah," Mr. Laurence says, "yes, indeed. We are good friends from school." I feel myself release a breath I had not realized I was holding. He turns to me. "But what were you doing in the cargo room, Mr. Hamilton?"

I pause. "Miss Dela's parents will not allow our marriage. I simply wished to be alone," I lie.

A smirk begins to cross his face, but he covers it with ease. In an instant, his eyes widen in shock and his jaw drops in sympathy. Oh, he is good.

"They will not consent? You must be joking! A strong, masculine man, such as you?" I scowl, his joke not lost on me. His mouth twitches, a smile hiding just beneath the surface. "They are both fools!"

"Precisely what I said!" the man adds. We both look at him and he takes the hint. Clearing his throat, he says, "Well, I must be getting back to work. Happy to be of service. Good luck with your lady, Mr. Hamilton." I nod in thanks. He tips his hat to us. "Good day."

"Good day," we echo. Once he has turned the corner, I finally look to Mr. Laurence. His smirk fills his face with light, those green eyes smoldering with amusement. He leans against the doorjamb, his arms folded before him. Not saying a word, he stares at me.

"What?" I finally ask, annoyed.

He shakes his head and begins to clap. "Bravo!"

"Oh, make quiet," I say, and playfully hit him in the arm.

He gasps. "Did Little-Miss-Proper-Young-Lady just tell me to 'make quiet'?"

"Yes, she did, and she meant it," I say, suppressing the urge to smile.

"Honestly, you put on a good show." He laughs. "Care to explain?"

"Not particularly, no."

"What a shame for you then," he says, before grabbing my arm, just as he had done before, and swinging me inside. I collapse to the same pink chaise. He closes the door and leans back against it, crossing his arms. A feeling of déjà vu passes through me. The footman hurries into the bedroom. Honestly, just how many girls does Mr. Laurence bring here?

"What is going on, Vi?"

"Nothing," I mumble. What can I tell him? Certainly not that I am one of the Others, one of the Marked. He already knows I am not who I pretend to be, but how much is too much of the truth?

"Why were you really in the cargo room?" he asks.

I do not answer, but rather stare at my hands in my lap.

Mr. Laurence sighs and sits down beside me. "I don't know why I helped you this morning," he says, "but I did. I could have handed you in, but I didn't."

"I know," I whisper.

"You are like a mystery I cannot solve. The girl who dresses as a boy, steals food, lies, and for reasons still unknown, spends her time in the cargo room. What is her story?"

I meet his eyes. "You would not like this story."

"Actually, mystery novels are precisely my cup of tea." He grins.

A meek smile forms at the corner of my mouth before I can restrain it. "Perhaps, but not this one."

"Well," he says, "what is it about?" Mr. Laurence leans

forward with his head cupped in his hands, his elbows balanced upon his knees. His head tilts up towards me, vibrant green waiting patiently to absorb my tale from underneath the dark fringe of his eyelashes.

Standing up, I begin to pace. You cannot tell him anything, El! Keep your mouth shut!

"A lying thief who pretends to be a boy, just as you said."

"And why does this lying thief who pretends to be a boy spend her time in the cargo room?" he asks. His gaze fixates on me, honest and true.

I smile and slowly back towards the door. "I suppose you will just have to buy the book," I say, and slip out into the hall.

I feel as though I might throw up, but it has nothing to do with being on the ship. It is the feeling that accompanies a lie, a feeling I have come to know all too well. How can I continue to lie to him again and again? Eventually, he will learn the truth and hate me forever.

"What do I care if Mr. Laurence hates me?" I ask no one in particular. Stop it, El. It does not matter anyway, I tell myself. The ship will be docking in a week and I will never have to lie to him again.

I sigh, knowing this time I am only lying to myself.

8
DREAMING

"Shall we play a game?" Dela chirps. She sits on the floor with her legs crossed, feasting on a slice of cranberry bread.

"That all depends. Which one do you wish to play?" I say.

Her brow furrows as she flips through the list of games in her head. "Hmm... Well, I suppose we cannot play Hide and Seek with all of these boxes, and Red Rover is out of the question. Why do we not make up a game?"

"Very well." We sit in silence. I stare at the ceiling again, pretending to think of ideas as I imagine the starry night just beyond the wooden planks. How beautiful it must be atop the ship, especially with summer just around the corner. Oh, how I do love spring! Just when you are sure winter has sucked the life out of all things, that first flower blooms, a tiny breath of green in a land of ice.

"Oh, I know!" Dela exclaims, jarring me out of my dreams. "We will play Truths!"

"Truths? What in the world is Truths?"

She glares at me impatiently. "I made it up, remember? We must ask each other questions, and we cannot lie when we answer. When you are asked a question you do not wish to answer, you can pass, but then you lose."

"That's not a game," I argue.

"It is now!" she says. "Here, I'll go first." She looks at me with those piercing blues and I already feel myself forming a lie. A devilish grin plays across her lips. "Who is Mr. Laurence?"

My face grows heated, a blush warming my cheeks and dotting my neck with red splotches. That conniving little... She was listening when I told that man to take me to Mr. Laurence! Are you allowed to pass on the very first question?

"You had this planned all along," I say, "from the moment you said, 'Let's play a game!'"

She smiles. "I have added a new rule. You cannot pass on the first question."

"Of course you have," I mumble, before relinquishing. With a sigh, I say, "Mr. Laurence is a gentleman I met when I went on deck." Reluctantly, I add, "He knows I am a girl."

"El! How could you?"

"It was an accident!" I yell in my defense. "My hat fell off!"

Her jaw sets firmly and her eyes narrow. Shame fills

my very being and I am utterly embarrassed by my actions. "You didn't tell him anything else, did you?"

"Of course not!"

Disapproval still holds her brows cocked far above her eyes, but she manages a terse "Good." I am forgiven this time.

We stare at one another, our secrets forming a bond even stronger than our sisterhood. Accident or not, I have made a dire mistake; I know it and Dela knows it. If Mr. Laurence is to learn any more of the truth, I will be betraying my sister as well as myself.

"This game is stupid. I'm going to bed and you should do the same," I say.

"But you have not asked me a question!"

"You got what you wanted out of the game, now go to sleep," I say through gritted teeth.

"But—"

"Go to sleep, Dela!"

I turn away. Lying down, I curl into a ball and rest my head on my arms. I hear Dela sigh and shuffle back over to her corner. An inkling of guilt seeps under my skin at the thought of my harsh words.

"Goodnight, El," she whispers.

The few bubbles of anger that still sputter around my conscience slowly begin to dissipate. It was a stupid fight, as are most of our arguments, and it is forgotten within minutes. Such is the way with sisters, I suppose. "Sweet dreams, Dela."

A few moments later I hear her call my name. "El?"

"Yes?"

"I miss Mother."

Me too, Dela. Me too.

I sit up and crawl over to where she lies. Tears flow down her face in smooth rivers of sorrow. "Don't cry, Dela. We will see them again soon, you'll see." She nods, though I know she believes me about as much as I do. Is lying still a bad thing if you do it for the right reasons? Is it wrong to lie to protect the ones you love?

I ask her another question to occupy her mind. "What did Mother do when you could not sleep?"

She shrugs. "When I was younger, she would give me a glass of warm milk and sing, but I am too old for that now, El."

I do not listen; I have already begun to sing a lullaby Mother used to sing to me.

"Rockaby, lullaby, bees in the clover,

Crooning so drowsily, crying so low."

Her eyes flutter shut. Her arm wraps around my waist and I drape an arm over her, as well.

"Rockaby, lullaby, dear little rover,

Down into wonderland..."

My voice fills the cargo room though it is little more than a whisper. Dela's breathing becomes drawn out and heavy; she is asleep. At ease, I close my eyes, allowing the song to fill my mind and carry me down into wonderland, too...

—

It begins with fire.
Red hot flames of terror, their blue cores pulsing as quickly as my heart.

I am alone, surrounded by Radicals.

"Elvira!"

Dela? The scene shifts and I see her soot-covered face as she stands between my parents in front of the field of grass. I try to run. Can't. Men grab from all sides, bringing me down, choking, tearing, laughing...

Another scene change: the men become molten fire on top of me. My skin burns and I scream, a primal scream that cannot possibly be coming from me. I see violet, pulsating and glowing on my wrist, but the Mark cannot save me. No one can save me! I am lost to the fire.

Dela appears, floating over me like a ghost. Reaching out a hand, I wait for her to pull me out of the fiery depths. Her mouth opens, unleashing a startling mix between a snarl and a cackle.

"Rockaby, lullaby, dear little rover,
Down into wonderland..." she sings.

She circles above me, laughing and giggling. "Down and down and down, El! Down you go!" she sing-songs.

"Ashes to ashes! Down into wonderland..."

Her face contorts, skin bubbling and melting into a new form, a new face; it is Scar-face.

"No escapin' me precious!" he sneers.

With a gasp, my eyes snap open and I escape, for now. The images of my nightmare flash before my eyes, more vivid and clear than reality. The room's blue shadows replace the fire and Radicals. Dela's soft snoring replaces her terrifying song.

Only a dream. A terrifying, horrific dream, but a dream all the same.

My skin is slick with cold sweat. My hair tangled around my head. I stand, wide awake and too afraid to fall back asleep. I pace.

What I would not do to escape this room! I stare at the door, the ceiling, the walls, picturing what lies just beyond. A black sky filled with millions of shimmering diamonds. Tempting, yes, but also risky. Very risky.

"Don't do it, El," I tell myself. "Don't do it."

I do not listen, my need for air and rebellion greatly overpowering logic and reason. Dela is asleep, the entire ship is asleep. No one will ever know about the girl with the Mark who sat on the deck gazing at stars.

9
WISHING

A close call with a couple in steerage has me on edge, but I make it to the top deck without any other such occurrences. I find a spot behind a lifeboat where I can see without being seen and nestle down. Leaning my head back, my eyes finally connect with what they have longed for these past two days. The smell of salt overwhelms the sweet memories of my flowers, but at least I have the sky.

An unexpected twang in my chest accompanies the image of my father, lying beside me, pointing at the stars. The memories of Mother scolding him for filling my head with dreams make me want to laugh and cry at the same time. I miss them, though I'll never allude as to how much.

I cling to hope with shaking hands. They are alive, I tell myself. How can they possibly be dead? Then again, I think, how can they not?

Last time I saw Father he was clutched in the grasp of a Radical, barely holding onto life, and Mother was saying her goodbyes. Was there a forever behind those words?

Did she think it was goodbye forever? Surely not.

Looking to the stars, I inhale deeply, cleansing my mind of horrid memories. I concentrate on the stars and the stars alone. Such stories Father used to tell about these stars. These same stars on this same sky, no different than the sky back home. My only connection to my life before. Before the Radicals. Before the war.

Anger boils in my blood. How naïve I had been back then, believing the war would never affect me. How could it? My family had done nothing terrible, right? Wrong. My family lived. I was too ignorant to see that I was not hated for something I had done but for something I was, something I am. The Mark on my wrist makes me different, and no one likes different. It frightens them. People like a world that makes sense, a world where everyone is the same, but nothing about us makes sense.

We have Marks, strange unusual Marks that blessed— or cursed—us with powers. Dela receives visits from spirits. A Mediator. I often see her laughing by herself in a corner or staring at invisible things just over my shoulder. But since this is the RMS *Celtic*'s maiden voyage, there is very little spiritual activity upon its decks; at least, that is what Dela tells me.

Mother and Father are Kinetics, able to move things without touching them. They can stop a cup of tea from toppling over onto the new rug, and Mother has always been fond of holding chocolates in the air before we finish our Latin lessons. Household chores, minor punishments, and conversing with ghosts: that is all they ever use their gifts for. But does any of it matter to the Radicals? Does it make any difference to them that I have no powers despite my Mark? No. If you are Marked, you are the enemy. If you are Marked, you are hated.

Hatred.

I did not believe such hatred and violence was capable before the war, but I see the truth now. We are vermin beneath their shoes, not human. We had always been shunned and disliked, but when one Marked killed a man with his powers, it was all the public needed to start a war. And now that war has been officially declared, there is nothing stopping them from squashing us like bugs beneath their soles.

Still, even as the war raged on, I was sure I was safe—safe in my little village, safe in my garden, safe under the canopy of stars. Such foolish certainty! No one is safe. I see that now. I see everything now.

Fuming with anger, I tear my gaze away from the sky. My eyes fall upon a new object of interest. A man sits on the bench across from where I rest, staring at me. I go rigid, terror making me immobile. It takes me a moment to fully process what I am seeing. It is so dark, but I can tell he is young with dark hair and... is he?—he is!—he is smirking at me! I gasp, realization crashing into me like a runaway carriage. How did I not hear him coming? How did I not see him?

Apparently, I see everything except him!

"Hello, Vi." His voice, so unexpected and loud against the still night, startles me. I fly into a standing position, backing against the rail of the ship. My hat topples off and I make to grab for it, but it is too late. It falls into the darkness and is consumed by the ocean.

"Damn it!" I exclaim, much louder than anticipated. Involuntarily, I put a hand to my mouth. Proper ladies do not swear under any circumstances: Mother's words so clear in my mind.

I still face the ocean, but I hear his soft chuckle. "Who would have thought you'd have such a foul mouth," he laughs. "Though don't worry about me. I love a lady with a bit of an edge." I grimace. God, I can just picture him winking!

I take only a moment to mourn the loss of my hat before returning to more important matters. I turn around, back against the rail, hands gripping it for support. Black curls envelop my face. They thrash around in the breeze, free at last. I feel my violet eyes burning with questions, but I say nothing. I simply stare, mouth agape.

"Sorry about your hat. I didn't mean to startle you." Mr. Laurence smiles and bites his lip as he walks forward. "Well, no, that's not exactly true. I did mean to startle you." He chuckles. "I just failed to realize how well it would work!"

Annoyance replaces my shock. I find my voice. "What are you doing out here?"

He spreads his arms, placating. "I was stalking you, of course. What about you?" he asks. "A bit of late night stargazing?"

I cross my arms. "Why are you really out here?"

He raises a finger, wiggling it back and forth as he says, "Ah, ah, ah. I answer a question when you answer a question. Why were you really in the cargo room?" My lips are sealed; no more secrets shall pass them. I do not answer. I stare into his eyes, waiting for something to betray him—a flinch, a wink—but I see only amusement and curiosity. He groans as he looks to the sky, squeezing his eyes shut. "Why must you be so aggravating?"

"I should ask you the same question," I mumble.

"Well," he says, ignoring me, "since I am above begging, I will leave the subject alone for now." As he speaks, he walks languidly—closer and closer to where I stand until he is only a foot away.

He looks at me and then at the stars. Turning around, he gazes, seemingly transfixed, at the sky before he circles back to his starting point and looks down at me.

"I don't understand," he says.

His words take me by surprise. "What do you mean you do not understand?"

He sighs as though speaking to a child. "I do not understand your fascination with the stars, that's all.

You seemed absolutely mesmerized by them when I was watching you from the bench."

I pull myself tighter against the rail. "You were watching me?" How long exactly had he been sitting there?

"Do you not listen? I told you I was stalking you," he says, another infamous smirk making its way onto that perfectly tan face.

A scowl creases my brow in what I am sure is an extremely unattractive expression. "Well, I must be getting back," I say. I make to step by him, but he moves faster. My body is thrust back against the bars of the rail and his presses closer. His arms straddle my waist on either side, gripping the bar and butting up against my own hands. I feel the sudden warmth of his proximity and butterflies swarm in my stomach. A wave of annoyance at my reaction mixes with my frustration towards him.

"Please, don't leave," he breathes. "I didn't mean to offend you."

Air turns solid in my lungs. I feel those green eyes—so startlingly light—trying to find mine. Looking everywhere but at him, I simply nod. He takes a moment to back away. With a deep breath, I finally lift my gaze.

His back is turned to me now as he walks away, moving towards the bench. He takes off his morning coat and twirls it in his hand. Halfway to the bench, he stops and to my surprise, flops down on his back in the middle of the deck. I stare at him, tilting my head to the side like an inquisitive puppy.

He cranes around to look at me and then lies back down. He loosens his blue tie and unbuttons the top two buttons of his collar. Taking off his top hat, he places it on his stomach and pushes up his sleeves. An arm stretches out and pats the spot beside him. He must be joking! I cannot lie down there! I would be out in the open for anyone to see.

As though reading my mind, he says, "I don't know why you found it necessary to hide behind that lifeboat. It is the middle of the night. No one will see us."

Reluctantly, I walk over to where he lies. I stand there, my feet at his waist, and look down at him. He closes his eyes and drums his fingertips on the top of his hat.

"Lie down," he murmurs.

"B-but it isn't proper," I say.

He opens one eye. "It isn't proper for a lady. However, you are no longer a lady, correct?"

"I suppose... but—"

"No 'buts'. Be a man," he asserts, patting the space beside him a second time. The superior tone of his voice infuriates me and I sit to prove that he is no better than I am. I spread out on the deck, unfolding like an accordion, parallel to Mr. Laurence.

I turn my head to the side to see him. A smile tugs at the corner of his lips and I smile, too. Facing forward again, I look at the black expanse above us. It glitters with billions of tiny specks, each one a part of something so much larger than itself. The stunning beauty of it makes me grin.

"Wish upon a star, Vi," he whispers.

I close my eyes. So many wishes, desires, wants, and needs burn beneath the purple expanse of my eyelids as I concentrate on the image of the blue star I have secluded from the rest. I wish... I wish my family was together again. I wish I could go back to my garden. I wish Father was here to tell me stories and whisper promises of better days. I wish there was no war. No Radicals. No hatred... No Marks.

I wish...

I feel him staring at me and look over. He is watching me, just as I thought. A smile spreads across his face.

"What?" I ask in a shaky laugh.

His grin widens. The green of his eyes penetrates me. I stare harder, noticing the outer ring of blue and the speckles of silver reflected in the moonlight. He turns away, shaking his head as he continues to smile.

I laugh again. "What are you smiling at? Tell me."

"You really love it, don't you? Gazing at the stars," he says. I look away, knowing we are verging on something personal. "In all of our encounters you appear so tense, as though you have a hundred different things on your mind, but when you look at the stars," he pauses, "your face glows with this unexplainable radiance. It is as though the world just melts away. All of your worries, your fears: gone."

As he speaks, I cannot help gawking. It is as though someone has crawled inside my mind and is telling me all of the feelings I could never explain. He looks back at me with a timid smile. Our eyes meet, a new connection I hadn't experienced before.

I clear my throat and break eye contact. "My father and I used to lie in my garden together every night and look at the stars. He told the most wonderful stories about the constellations. We would sit out there for hours, making up stories and listening to each other breathe." I pause. "It's odd, isn't it? How comforting the sound of someone breathing beside you can be?"

He does not speak for a while, as though lost in his own thoughts. "Yes, I suppose it is."

We lie in silence, listening to each other's steady breathing. His low voice cuts through the quiet, but this time it is as smooth as velvet, melding into the silence without disturbing it.

"I should like to create a story," he whispers, almost to himself, before looking over with a devilish grin. "Would you make one up with me?"

He jumps into his tale without waiting for an answer. "It is about a girl and a boy," he says, "who meet in the most unusual circumstances." He raises his hand and begins to outline the shapes of a boy and a girl, connecting the stars one by one. The images come to life in my head. The faint outline formed by the stars and Mr. Laurence's probing finger supply the base as I fill in the finer details with a little imagination.

"What sort of circumstances?" I ask, playing along, though I am sure I already know the ending.

"You see, the girl was a criminal, a thief. She stole a loaf of bread from a crazed storeowner who chased her with a pickaxe!"

I smile. "You have a wild imagination. A pickaxe, honestly?"

"Oh, yes. The largest pickaxe in the world. The girl ran as hard as she could, but the man was gaining on her. She was sure she was going to die when a handsome, intelligent, humorous, brave boy came out of nowhere. Naturally, the boy saved the girl from the crazed pickaxe-wielding storeowner."

"Naturally," I murmur.

"The girl and the boy met again on numerous other occasions, but she was a very secretive girl. He began making ridiculous assumptions in his head. Perhaps she is a prostitute, he thought—"

I gasp, appalled. "Of course she's not!"

Mr. Laurence looks to me with a lopsided smile. "He came to the conclusion that none of his assumptions fit this girl. She was special, he knew that, and he knew that he would do anything to discover her secrets."

"Anything besides begging," I say, smirking.

He laughs. "But of course."

"And how does this story end?" I ask.

He shakes his head. "It is 'To Be Continued...'"

I sit up suddenly and turn to look at him. "No happy ending? You are an awful storyteller."

With a hand pressed to his chest, he opens his mouth in mock bewilderment as he sits up straight. "Dear me," he says. "That cuts deep, Vi. My heart may be eternally bruised from such an affront. You cannot possibly judge my abilities when I have not even finished."

I cross my arms. "Very well. Finish," I declare.

He crosses his arms, mimicking me, and I hastily drop my arms to my sides. "I cannot finish when I do not yet know the ending," he says, "though I can assure you the girl will tell the boy all there is to know about her very soon."

Don't count on it.

"As for the rest," he sighs, lying back down and tucking his hands under his head, "well, I suppose it all depends on the fate of the stars." He winks at me and closes his eyes. I shake my head in bewilderment and laugh. If nothing else, he never fails to surprise me. He is just so aggravatingly impudent and arrogant and... and yet, when I am in his company, it is as though the war and everything else disappears.

I lie back down, feeling the warmth radiating from his

fingertips resting only centimeters away from my hand. How easy it would be to just close that space...

A door bangs shut. We are both on our feet within seconds. I whip my head around, my hair flying in my face. My hair! My hat! I am ruined! Two shadowy figures move towards us, swaying and walking clumsily, pawing at one another to keep upright as they giggle.

"Vi!"

I turn. Fear of being discovered sends trembles up and down my body. Goosebumps rise on my arms. Mr. Laurence stands before me, his coat already back on and his tie tightened. A hand reaches out towards me. I take one more glance behind me at the approaching figures and without any more thought, put my pale hand in his tan one. His tight grip shocks me as he pulls me after him.

We run across the deck together, hand in hand, towards a door. Without hesitation, Mr. Laurence steps inside and continues running down the hall. We come to a corner and just as we are about to round it, he turns back against me, pinning my back against the wall. His hand still holds mine; his other is flat against the wall next to my head. His breathing is short. I suck in sweet air, happy for the oxygen in my lungs. His eyes dart excitedly, radiating with adrenaline.

"I finally understand your love of secrets," he whispers between panting. Hot breath caresses my face. "It is exciting, isn't it? Does a bloody good job of getting one's heart hammering!" He smiles and I cannot help but smile back.

He inclines his head to the corner, pressing his body closer. "There is a man around the corner," he whispers before taking another peek, "and he isn't leaving."

My blood pumps even faster. That man cannot see me. No one can see me, not with my hair hanging down around my face. I lean my head back and close my eyes, preparing to wait.

"I suppose we will just have to go past him," Mr. Laurence says casually. My eyes snap open. I open my mouth to argue, but he holds one warm finger to my lips and I am instantly quieted. Taking his hand out of my own, I am temporarily wounded before he reaches up and takes off his hat. In one fluid motion, he places it atop my head. "I owe you one, anyway," he says with a grin.

I take it off and wrap my hair up, securing the curls against my head. Quickly, I put the hat back on. I peek out from under the brim at him.

"Well," I whisper, "how do I look?"

He reaches out a hand, catching a flyaway curl and tucking it beneath the top hat. My face burns bright red and I lower my gaze in embarrassment. "Like an extremely feminine man," he says seriously.

I scowl, pursing my lips. He chuckles under his breath and pushes me out into the open hallway. He follows after me in his relaxed gait, hands tucked in pockets. We walk down the hallway, moving closer and closer to the man. I twitch, the urge to run screaming in my heart and in the tips of my toes. The man wears a dark suit with an elegant tail coat. His stiff collar brushes against his chin. As we walk by, he fixes a cold glare on us. I shiver, but Mr. Laurence is positively serene.

"Good night, sir," he says.

The man snorts. "Good night," he scoffs. "Not when we have disgusting leeches running amuck on the ship," he mumbles under his breath.

Mr. Laurence pauses beside me. He turns back to the man, his brow furrowed. "Leeches?" he inquires.

"Indeed. Apparently, several Marked snuck onto the *Celtic*, some in steerage, others hiding in the boiler room. A group of men was assembled to hunt them down, including myself." He spits each word, biting the ending syllable off of each one with his rage.

I feel the blood drain from my face. I am frozen where I stand, my violet eyes wide as saucers. They know. They know we are on the ship. They know and they are hunting us down. Dela. Have they found her yet? My knees knock together as I struggle to keep standing. This isn't happening! My legs give out beneath me, but Mr. Laurence's arms sweep under me before I can connect with the ground. I lean against him, needing his strength to keep me from tumbling into hysterics.

"Vi?" he whispers in my ear, alarm shadowing his

face. I cannot answer. He wraps one of my arms over his shoulders and begins walking around the next corner. He shouts over his shoulder. "No worries! Lad simply had a bit too much to drink. Nothing a bit of sleep cannot cure! Good luck with your endeavor!"

The man calls after us, pumping his clenched fist in the air. "We will get them! Every last one of those wretched leeches! We have already killed two found in steerage; it is not long before we find the others! Long live the Radicals!"

Two already caught. Not long before...

My knees give way again and I collapse to the floor.

"Elvira?" His voice—it sounds so far away. I am lifted, two strong arms holding me against a warm chest. Shock and fear overpower my will. My eyes flutter shut as I slip under.

I wish...

—

The weight of the man's words press down on me even in sleep.

Not long before we find the others.

Not long at all.

10
KNOWING

In and out of consciousness, I travel between dream and reality until it is not long before the two are indiscernible. Voices fill my head. Dream? Reality? I am not sure.

"Is she awake yet?" a man asks, distress coloring his tone.

"Calm down, my dear. Give the girl time." It is a woman speaking. Something cool presses against my forehead; the cold, soft fabric feels wonderful on my hot skin.

"Give her time? She could be in a coma for all we know! We must wake her!"

"No!" The voice is gentle, but stern. "She must sleep. Something has clearly traumatized the dear girl."

"Very well," the man says. "I will stay with her. Please, get some sleep."

"No. I have had my sleep. You, my son, have been awake all night, no doubt gallivanting around with this young lady. You sleep; I will awake you when she rouses."

A sigh followed by a door slamming shut assures me the man has left. Without reluctance, I slip back into oblivion.

—

When I wake again, I force my eyes open. Light assaults my vision, blinding me. I squeeze my eyes shut as swirls and dots blink in and out of existence. My head feels light and I wait for it to subside before cautiously prying my eyes open a second time. Better accustomed to the brightness, images slowly form before me.

A large bed beneath me and a white comforter pulled up to my chin, soft as the most expensive furs. Green wallpaper and paintings of important-looking men adorn the walls. A chair to my left occupied by a man. His head bent, his hat lowered over his eyes. I watch his chest rise and fall in a slow cadence. How different Mr. Laurence appears with those astounding green eyes closed and his usual smirk relaxed into a straight line.

I consider waking him, but instead decide to slip out unnoticed. It is better this way, I tell myself, as I move through the bedroom door and into the drawing room. I have been a fool these past two days, fraternizing with the enemy, putting both my sister's and my own life at stake. Well, no more. One purpose pushes me forward, and that is to find Dela and get her safely to America. And whether

I like it or not, my promise to her and my mother does not involve Mr. Laurence.

Tiptoeing over the beautiful Persian rug, I walk around the pink chaise and reach the door. A silk hat hangs limply from an ornate coat rack. A twinge of shame knots my stomach as I lift the hat from its perch. There is no denying that I am a thief now, I think as I put it on and reach for the door.

My hand rests upon the doorknob, but I cannot will myself to open it. I take one more glance around the cabin, reluctant to leave its warmth and protection, afraid by what I might find back in the cargo room—or worse, what I might not find. What if Dela has already been caught?

With this thought in mind, I pull the door open, preparing to rush down to the cargo room, when a voice makes me stop.

"Miss Hamilton!" A hint of surprise threads through the woman's voice. Another person who knows my secret. Wonderful.

Slowly, I turn around.

A slender woman, wearing a pale blue dress that creates the S-curve silhouette every girl so desperately wishes to have, stares at me from across the room. The dress's sleeves puff out over her arms before coming to a halt at the lacey cuffs. Beautiful white lace drapes over her full low bust and creeps up into the stiff, high-boned collar. Beads are elegantly threaded into the hem of the dress. The crystals glitter as she steps closer, the hem brushing the floor and rippling with her movement. A sash encompasses her narrow waist and a broad-brimmed hat trimmed with colorful feathers and a stuffed hummingbird completes the ensemble. I feel myself sigh at its beauty, knowing I will never be able to afford something so lovely.

I force myself to raise my gaze, looking the fashionable woman in the eye. Her pink lips are pursed in a pleasant smile that stretches her skin and laugh lines wrinkle around her aged green eyes.

"Miss Hamilton, correct?" she says. I cannot speak. Words cower behind the swollen weight of my tongue. "Is that not your name?"

I nod. She smiles, continuing to move forward.

"I am sure you have already guessed who I am. I am Adam's mother, Mrs. Laurence," she says. "I am sorry we had to meet under such conditions."

Conditions? Conditions as in me being unconscious and carried here by her son? Or conditions as in me trying to slip out of their cabin unnoticed with a stolen hat? What a wonderful first impression I have made, I think.

"Would you be so kind as to close that door? I would very much like to speak with you if you don't mind." Her voice is innocent and pleasant. I surrender to the power of her authority and do as she asks. I close the door and sit down on the chaise. Mrs. Laurence sits down opposite me in a large winged chair.

She stares at me, her green eyes not prying for answers, but keenly interested. An awkwardness surrounds me in its chilling cloak. It makes me want to itch at my skin, as though it is an irritation I can soothe just by raking my fingernails across it. But instead, my hands are iron fists at my sides. The skin stretched taught over the white of my knuckles. I wait for her to speak.

Another smile lights her face as she says, "My son tells me you took quite the fall earlier."

I search for my voice. "I suppose I did, yes."

"You two were speaking to a man when it happened?" she inquires.

I shift uncomfortably in my seat. There it is again. That unexplainable itch, pricking its way across my arms, my thighs, my back. I nod.

"By the sound of it, this man was a Radical."

What is she playing at? What does she know? I can feel her leading up to something, probing around the matter that truly occupies her mind before she strikes.

"I believe so, yes," I say. "He was talking to us."

"About?"

"About the Marked," I whisper, my voice cracking on the last syllable.

A smile spreads up her face and into her eyes. I know we have finally reached what she truly wishes to discuss.

"And that was when you fainted?"

"Yes, but I was simply light-headed. I had a long day. I

was tired and I hadn't eaten much." The excuses fly out of my mouth and I am helpless to stop them.

Mrs. Laurence leans forward, her kind eyes full of sympathy and knowledge. "I know, Elvira."

Time freezes. My heart stops in my chest. I feel the blood cease pumping. I feel my breath halt in the middle of exhaling. Green eyes fix on my violet ones. My body is rigid. Unable to move. Frozen. Only one thing moves freely through the suddenly icy world. My voice. Slow and quiet, it whispers a question, so innocent and full of pain.

"You know?" My voice falters. My throat aches. My hands tremble.

She nods solemnly. "I know why you fainted when you saw the Radical." She pauses. "I know what you are."

The world unfreezes, flooding in, snapping back, and collapsing down on top of me in one fell swoop. She knows. She knows! My promise to Dela crumbles with those two words. She knows!

"When Adam brought you to me, you were feverish. Your breathing was shallow and I wanted to get your pulse," she whispers. "That was when I saw the Mark."

The reality of the situation hits me with a punch to the stomach and I crack. Cupping my face in my hands, I begin to sob. Tears stream down my cheeks in a torrent. My lungs clamp shut and the deep quavering gulps I struggle to take seem to carry no oxygen. It is all my fault. She knows! Dela and I will be handed over to the

Radicals. We will be killed. Thrown overboard. And it is all my fault!

"Please," I whisper, but so softly she does not hear. "Please, don't turn me in. Please. Please."

A hand wraps around my back as I cry and I shrink away before realizing it does not mean to hurt me. The woman beside me gazes at my tearful eyes and smiles in sympathy, attempting to soothe me as she combs her fingers through my hair and rubs my back. I stare at her in a mix of shock and confusion.

"Don't cry, my darling," she whispers. "It will be all right."

I wipe at my eyes. "I don't understand," I stutter.

She draws back in puzzlement. Her brow furrows. "Understand what, darling?"

"You know," I say as though it is the most obvious answer. "You know I am Marked."

She smirks, brushing a finger over my cheek. "Not everyone hates the Marked, my dear." And her touch, so kind, so gentle, instantly begins to calm me.

"You won't turn me in?" I ask, my bottom lip still quivering.

She shakes her head. The feathers on her hat flutter as she moves. "Heavens, no. However, I must ask you to be honest with me, Miss Hamilton."

I nod. This woman, this sole person who knows my deepest darkest secret, has given me a kind charity.

Having only known her for a few minutes, I trust her. I trust her with all my heart.

"Where were you hiding?" she asks.

"The cargo room," I answer, "with my sister."

She frowns. "Your sister?"

"Yes. Dela. She is twelve. She is still there." I hope.

Mrs. Laurence stands and begins to pace. "Very well. You will fetch her and bring her back here. The two of you will stay here until the ship docks in New York."

I shake my head. "I cannot do that, Mrs. Laurence. I will not put you and Mr. Laurence at risk."

"Don't you worry about us. No one doubts my authority, and my son has a way of talking his way out of every possible situation." She chuckles lightly as she says this. "We will be just fine. You will get your sister and bring her here. We will say you two are my nieces. Yes, nieces. That will do." She nods to herself as she forms the plan, assured it will work. "Go, now, before Adam awakes. Go. Go!"

Hastily, I move towards the door and make to step outside, but pause. Frozen in the middle of the doorway, I turn. Mrs. Laurence stares at me. Her loving eyes fall upon me as though I am truly her niece. My heart swells in adoration for this woman. I shift on the balls of my feet, afraid of the answer to my question.

My head lowered, I twiddle with a frayed end on my sleeve. "Are you sure, Mrs. Laurence? I would understand.

You don't have to do this."

"Yes," she says, and then smiles, "yes I do."

I smile and turn to leave, but her voice pulls me back. "Miss Hamilton," she calls.

"Yes?"

"Let your secret remain between you and me. Mr. Laurence does not need to know." The look in her eyes stops me from opening my mouth to ask why. I nod and let the questions die inside me.

I slip through the door as I had done so many times before, knowing that I will return soon and knowing that this time, I will be welcomed.

11
INTRODUCING

By the time I reach the cargo room, I am drenched in sweat. I take deep breaths but the terrifying possibilities that lurk beyond the door, paired with a long sprint, leaves me gasping for air.

She could be gone, I think. I could open this door, and she could be gone. What then?

Shoving these thoughts into the back of my mind, I push through the door. My chest clenches. Menacing shadows hover over me, the crates becoming dark creatures rather than the mundane objects of reality. I peer into the darkness.

"Dela?" I call. "Dela, it's me! Dela?"

Terror knits into my chest, a colorful threadwork of worry and panic. A shrill undertone creeps into my voice. "Oh, Dela, please be here," I whisper as I step deeper into the room.

Something moves to my right and I freeze. Another flash of movement and my heart picks up momentum.

A form takes shape behind one of the crates. I open my mouth to scream, to cry for help, when the blur of movement suddenly turns into a familiar figure. My sister.

She runs forward, a shadow with bouncing golden curls, and slams into me. I stumble back with her sudden weight. She sobs against my chest, her thin arms wrapping tightly around my waist. Embracing her, I smile with relief.

"I—I was so afraid, El. I woke up and you were gone. You were gone and the Radicals—they were here, looking for us! They were so close to finding me, El! They were so close, but something made them leave. I was hiding just back there." She points to the furthest corner. She raises her gaze, accusing blue discs in search of answers. "How could you leave me, El? How could you do that? I was so frightened. I was so terribly frightened."

Despite her words, I know she is too relieved to see me to be truly angry.

"Everything is all right. I am here now. We're together and we are safe. Everything is all right," I murmur into her hair.

She pulls away. Tears create luminescent circles under her eyes. "Everything is not all right, El. They will be back. I overheard them talking. They've already searched the boiler room and steerage. And it is not as though there will be an empty room in first-class for us to hide away in. We have nowhere else to go."

I smile, reveling in my knowledge. "Yes, we do." A devious smirk plucks at the corner of my lips and my eyes betray me.

"What do you know that I don't?" she asks, eyeing me suspiciously. She shifts then, the set of her eyes changing with a new thought. "Why do I have a terrible feeling this has something to do with that man you have been sneaking off to see?"

I scowl, but ignore her comment. Taking hold of her hand, I lead her back to the door. "Come with me."

We trail out into the hallway and both glance back at the cargo room. I smile down at her and she smiles back as we both share the same thought: This is goodbye. Our time among the crates is over now. Never again will we have to sleep in their company. Yes. A goodbye to the past and a hello to whatever awaits us. I cannot help but think that everything is going to be different now.

Everything.

—

"Would you like some tea, Mrs. Laurence?"

A maid hovers over the woman sitting across from me. Dela sits beside me, her foot bouncing against the floor and making the whole chaise vibrate with the movement.

I put a hand on her knee. The bouncing ends and she

glances at me sheepishly.

"Yes, tea would be lovely. Thank you, Gertrude," Mrs. Laurence says.

"And for the girls?" Gertrude asks, inclining her head towards us. "Would you two care for some tea?"

"No, thank you," I say at the same time Dela says, "Yes, please."

We both turn to each other, her expression full of confusion and incredulity. "But, El! You love tea!"

"I'm not thirsty," I say through clenched teeth. It feels wrong, accepting tea from this woman who has already given us so much. How could I possibly take anything more?

"But—"

I silence her with a glare. Grudgingly, she turns her attention away from me as she gazes around the room. I follow her line of sight, from the stunning paintings in their golden frames to the Morris Company chair mother always dreamed about. The dragon design carved into the mahogany seems to truly breathe fire.

"This is a beautiful cabin, Mrs. Laurence," Dela says.

Mrs. Laurence looks around, as though just noticing its beauty. "That is very kind of you to say. Thank you."

For a moment, I am most pleased with Dela's behavior, before she says, "It must have cost a fortune."

I slam my heel down on her toe as I send her another piercing glare, but she simply continues. "Do you own a car, too? Vi wishes to own a car, but I personally—"

I shoot out of my seat so fast the chaise jerks back as though cowed by my intensity. "Dela!" I chide.

Her innocent blue eyes find mine. Mrs. Laurence chuckles and I gaze at her dubiously.

"Oh, it is quite all right, Miss Hamilton. I admire young women who are not afraid to speak their minds. Should women not say what they feel just because it is not viewed as proper? The prejudices against women are not all too different from the prejudices against the Marked, Miss Hamilton. You would be wise to remember that."

An apology forms in my mind, but before I can utter it, a door slams shut. Our attention snaps towards the source of the sound and my stomach skips into my throat. Standing just outside the bedroom door is Mr. Laurence. His hair is tousled, ends sticking out at odd angles. One side of his shirt is untucked and his tie twists over one shoulder. As he steps forward, I realize his feet are bare against the carpet.

"Mother, it's Elvira. She has—" His voice fills with urgency before his gaze settles on me. "Oh," he whispers, his crazed green eyes seeming to calm with this single word.

Mrs. Laurence stands and Dela follows. "Good morning, my darling. I was just getting to know your new friend. The cabin she has been staying in is, unfortunately, infested with rats. I have offered her a place in our cabin and she has graciously accepted."

He nods as she speaks, his gaze flaring with her last words, but I cannot read his expression. "Yes, that sounds reasonable."

Dela stands on the tips of her toes to reach my ear and whispers, "I forgive you. I would have snuck off to see him, too, if I were you."

Without a word, I pinch her arm. She smiles tightly as she turns to Mr. Laurence. "Are you going to introduce me or not, El?" she says, loud enough for all to hear.

Her words make me jump, and I blink rapidly as though awakened from a strange dream. "Yes, of course. Mr. Laurence, may I introduce my sister, Dela Hamilton. Dela, this is Mr. Laurence." Secretly, I hold my breath, waiting for her sure-to-be-embarrassing reply.

"Pleasure to make your acquaintance, Dela," he says, pressing his lips against the top of her hand. Her cheeks flare bright red and I roll my eyes, suppressing a giggle. When he rises, he turns to me. "You never told me you had a sister, Vi."

"Adam!" Mrs. Laurence barks. "I am terribly sorry, Miss Hamilton. My son has an aversion to using anything besides one's Christian name."

I smile. "He also seems quite fond of creating nicknames," I say as we all laugh at his expense.

Mrs. Laurence glances at the door and sighs. "My sincere apologies, but I really must be going. I promised

Mrs. Lindell I would accompany her to morning tea."

"Ah, yes, I remember," Mr. Laurence says, stepping closer.

"You will also remember that there is a ball tonight. We all must be in attendance," she says. Looking around the room, she calls for Gertrude.

The old woman appears from the bedroom. "Yes, Mrs. Laurence?"

"If you could please draw a bath and assist the girls in bathing and dressing."

"Of course, Mrs. Laurence," she says before departing into the bathroom.

I glance at Mr. Laurence, entreating him with my eyes to say something. He clears his throat, shuffling forward on his bare feet. "I am sure Vi is quite capable of bathing herself, Mother."

"I don't need any help either!" Dela whines.

She glances between us hesitantly, but eventually throws her hands in the air. "Oh, very well, but I expect you both to smell like a dozen roses when I return!" she laughs before slipping through the door.

Gertrude sneaks out from the bathroom in silence. "The bath is ready now, Miss Hamilton. Who shall go first?"

"I want to go first!" Dela says, running past the older woman into the bathroom. The door slams shut behind her and I stop myself from scolding my sister for her evident lack of propriety. A groan wells up inside of me; I am becoming my mother.

Gertrude looks to me for confirmation. I shrug. "She is dirtier than I."

As I say this, Dela's blonde head pokes out from behind the door. "Am not!"

Beside me, Mr. Laurence shakes his head in disbelief. I look to him questioningly.

"Splendid," he mumbles, a playful seriousness glinting in his eyes. "Just what the world needs. Two Vi's."

12
TELLING

I wait in the bedroom as Dela bathes. Pulling back the white bedspread, I slip under and haul it up to my chin. I close my eyes, playing through all of the events that had brought me to this moment.

I try to picture Mr. Laurence's face when he found out I would be staying with him and his mother. Did he seem pleased? Was he angry? I can't be sure and asking him would be unbearable. I roll over onto my stomach, wanting to block him from my mind—a task that has become increasingly difficult.

At the thought of not wanting to think about him, my mind naturally fills with images and memories of Mr. Laurence. With a groan, I turn back onto my side and open my eyes. Bright green irises and a blinding white grin stare back at me. I scream. Shocked, I jump back, falling over the edge of the bed and tumbling onto the floor. In an attempt to stand, I grab hold of the bedside; it teeters with the pull of my weight.

I hold a hand to my heart, waiting until my breathing slows. I look back to the bed; he still lies there, not perturbed by my outburst in the least. His smile stretches as I glower at him. Shifting onto his side, he props himself up on one elbow. His hand cradles his ego-filled head.

"Adam!" I shriek.

A chuckle vibrates deep in his throat, and a glint in his eyes puts me on edge.

"What?" I ask cautiously.

His smile turns into a smug smirk. "You called me Adam."

I open my mouth to argue when I realize he is right. I did call him Adam. I called him Adam! Never before has using one's Christian name seemed to carry so many implicit insinuations. Still, not wanting to admit it was an accident, I feign indifference. With a roll of my eyes, I say, "That is your name, is it not?"

He shakes his head. I should have known he would see right through me. "You called me Adam," he taunts.

Slowly, I move towards the bed as I cross my arms over my chest. "Mr. Laurence, if you would please—"

He does not let me finish. "Oh, come on, Vi. Have we not passed the formal name stage of our relationship? Are we not friends?"

The question catches me off guard. I take a step back, tucking my hair behind my ears. I look to him, wanting to study his expression, to see if he is only playing with me, but his face is perfectly composed.

"I—I don't know. Are we?"

The corner of his mouth lifts in a crooked smirk. "I asked you first."

I turn around, unable to look him in the eye as I say, "I wouldn't be able to say. Dela and I grew up in a small village on the outskirts of Liverpool. There weren't a lot of children there."

The bed squeaks as Adam moves to stand. I feel the heat of his body, suddenly very close to mine. His breath warms the back of my neck , and at the same time, sends chills running down my spine. I refuse to turn around, to get caught in the hypnosis of his gaze.

"Are you trying to tell me you never had any friends?" he breathes. His voice is like a deep purr, coaxing the answer out of me. I want to answer. I want to tell him everything, before he adds, "Because that is truly pathetic."

I spin around on my heel, a sudden anger controlling my body rather than my brain. Unbalanced, I reach out to steady myself against his chest and instantly rip my hands back, appalled. He laughs at my reaction; my agitation grows.

"I never said I didn't have any friends," I spit.

"Fine, Vi. Who, then, were your friends?"

I open my mouth, but do not have a reply. He is right. That is exactly what I was trying to say. I do not know what it is to have a human friend. There were few Marked children in our village, and all were much younger than Dela or I. As for those without Marks? Not many chose to live in a village infested with Marked. The few that did wouldn't dare allow their children to play with us.

Yet Dela still managed to have friends; they just weren't alive. Despite being ghosts, they offered all a real friend would provide as she ran around the house playing Hide and Seek, Red Rover, and Hopscotch. Meanwhile, I entertained myself.

"My friends were the flowers," I whisper. It is only when his finger slips under my chin, tilting my face upwards so that I must gaze into his eyes, that I realize I just spoke aloud. "I liked to pretend that they talked to me. The roses would always complain about the old man's beards and dandelions that were trying to conquer their land. I made believe that I was their savior. I would pluck out all of the weeds, and the Gladioli would shower me with thanks and they would make me a woven crown of Genistra and Leptospermum. Then at night, we would have a grand feast and dance beneath the stars. They were my only friends, Adam." My voice fades out until it is barely audible.

As I speak, I do not resist his hand beneath my jaw, nor do I resist his smoldering gaze. He watches me, watches my lips as I tell him about my garden, watches my eyes as they flicker across his face, and watches my cheeks as they develop a rosy glow. He breathes in my story without a word, and when I finish, he does not laugh.

"How many people have you told about the flowers?" he whispers.

I think about it for a moment, then smile. "No one."

"Then it is a secret?" he asks.

"Yes," I say. "I suppose it is."

His hand moves out from beneath my chin, drawing its way up my jaw, and capturing a black curl between his fingers. He stares at it absently as he twirls it in his hand. I hold my breath. Glowing with a new fire, those green eyes travel over my face until they connect with the violet of my own. Slowly, he leans forward. I stare at his lips, watching them as they inch closer and closer to mine.

My mind screams for me to do something. It hollers for me to stop him from moving any closer, but I am frozen. My lungs cry for air; I breathe in through my nose. His lips part only an inch from my own, where they pause. I close my eyes as he moves past my mouth to just above my neck. With his warm breath caressing my ear, my thoughts dissolve into a fog. Its haze intermingles with his sweet breath. Though his lips never touch my skin, the possibility is frighteningly present. I keep my eyes shut, still hesitant to breathe.

"I told you, you would tell me your secrets," he murmurs. "Chapter one of the story that is Elvira Hamilton," he breathes in my ear and slowly brings his face in front of mine. His thumb brushes across the fading cut on my cheek, still imprinted with the fire of that hideous night. A smirk lights his features. His nose wrinkles on one side. It is amazing how a smile upon his face can instantly eradicate all of my thoughts, my fears. The grin broadens as he says, "And I didn't even have to buy the book."

I stand there in shock, unable to move or speak. The bedroom door is pushed open and we both look to see Gertrude standing in the entrance. She looks curiously from Adam to me and back again, her eyes narrowing as she looks at the thin space between us. We both back away.

"Miss Dela is done in the lavatory, Miss Hamilton. I have drawn another bath for you," she says, and then adds purposefully, "if you are done here."

If I am done? As if I can be finished with something that has never begun. The moment—whatever it was—is gone. There will not be an opportunity for another. Adam and I? It's simply impossible; I might as well accept it now before it has the ability to pain me any more than it already does.

I grin, glancing back at Adam as I move to the door. "Yes, quite done. Thank you, Gertrude."

"Of course, Miss Hamilton. Call when you are ready to dress."

I nod and she exits the room with a sly glance back over her shoulder at the two of us. I turn back to the room; Adam stands before me. I jump, putting a slender hand to my mouth as I emit a yelp.

"You really must stop doing that," I hiss.

"And miss out on all the fun? Never."

I turn in the direction of the bathroom, but he grabs my arm, pulling me back.

His eyes latch onto me, searching. "Your secret is safe with me, Vi. Any secret of yours is safe with me. I hope you know that. I hope you know that you can trust me."

"If you reveal your secrets to the wind, you should not blame the wind for revealing them to the trees," I whisper. "Kahlil Gibran."

"Well, Kala Gabron—"

"Kahlil Gibran," I correct him.

"The point is he does not know me." He pokes a finger at his chest. "I know me, and I know that this wind keeps his promises."

I meet his gaze and know that he speaks the truth, but I still cannot divulge my secrets to him. Even if I wished it, I cannot scrounge up what I have so well hidden in the deepest cavern of my heart. I cannot allow my mouth to spill these words I have forbidden it to say.

I nod. "I believe you," I whisper. "Sadly, it doesn't change anything."

He smiles. "For now," he declares. "Chapter two will come, Vi, and I will be waiting patiently until it does." He holds my gaze before lowering his eyes to his feet, still bare against the carpet. "The water will be getting cold;

you had best be going."

Shaking my head as though I can shake away the daze he has put me in, I walk out into the parlor.

"And by the way, Vi," he calls out. "You were wrong about me not liking this story. I was enthralled from page one!"

This is not the chapter I was afraid you would not like, Adam Laurence. You will not be so enthralled when you know the secret that marks my wrist in violet. You will not like the story then, and you certainly won't like me.

13
DISCOVERING

Swirling tendrils of steam rise from the surface of the water. A warm vapor hugs the bathroom walls and a misty fog coats the mirror above the sink. And although I cannot see my reflection in the mirror, a blurry image of a girl stares back at me from the surface of the water.

Her hair hangs limply around her face, black curls snarled around one another and twisted into troublesome knots. Smudges stand out against the pale white of her skin. Burning violet dances across the water. Like a window with the curtains pulled shut, her eyes are wide open, yet guarded.

Is this whom Adam sees? I wonder, scrutinizing my filthy face and wild hair, remembering that I have not bathed in over three days. A sudden afterthought troubles me even more: I must smell terrible!

Utterly embarrassed, I want to dip beneath the water and never come back out. I want to be able to wash away this feeling Adam has inflicted upon me along with the grime. If only it were that simple.

I dip a toe in the water and quickly retract before fully lowering myself into the bath. The water has cooled to the perfect temperature. A cake of soap rests on a dish by my shoulder, and I reach for it. It slips from my grasp, diving under the surface with a light splash. My hands trail the bottom of the tub—a claw-footed affair in the shape of an oval—in search of the silky feel of the escapee.

At last, I find it. Holding it firmly this time, I glide it over my body, scrubbing its suds deep into my skin and hair until the water has become gray with dirt and ash. I stare at the water's blackness and think back to standing on the beach that night. As I remember the distraught cries that floated across the dark expanse, still distinctly ringing in my ears, I snap back to the present.

I stand in a flourish; water rises with me, but unable to defy gravity, slides back down my body and into the murky pool. Grabbing a blue silk robe as I step out of the bath, I slip it onto my shoulders. I look around the space for my clothes, but the dirty trousers and shirt are gone, a few specks of debris the only sign that they were ever there.

Figuring that Gertrude had taken them to be washed, I open the door a crack and call her name. I am not answered, and I step out farther into the living room, my wet hair dripping down my back. My left arm aches from keeping it pinned to my side, hiding the Mark. I pull the robe tighter as I look back and forth in search of the woman and my clothes. Annoyed, I turn back towards the door of the bathroom when I suddenly slam into Adam.

He stumbles backwards as I fall forward and knock us both to the ground. A stream of curses escapes his lips. I let out a groan as my elbow knocks against an end table. In a panic, I glue my wrist back to my side, terrified it is too late. Has it already been seen? Did he see it when we were falling?

My legs tangle around his, our chests press together. A silk robe is the only thing that separates us and I feel it slide against my skin as it creeps up my thigh. I raise my head to see his face. He holds a hand behind his head, groaning as he rubs the back of his skull. His eyes squeeze shut.

"Why did you run into me?" I say angrily.

His eyes finally snap open, the startling green making my breath catch as they ignite with an anger to match my own. "Me? Who's on top of whom here?"

"You're the one who snuck up behind me!"

"You're the one traipsing around here naked."

My eyebrows furrow together as my mouth drops open. I glance down at the thin robe wrapped around my body and am positively mortified. Why did I not just wait in the bathroom until Gertrude returned? "Gertrude. She—she took my clothes!"

I push myself up from him, making sure to keep

everything covered. I fold my arms over my chest. A quick glance down assures me that the Mark is fully concealed. Slowly, Adam stands and brushes himself off as he says, "That is why I was behind you. I was told to put these inside the bathroom door with strict orders about not looking at you, though I suppose that is all blown to pieces now..." He does not finish, but simply hands over what he had just picked up from the floor.

I take one glance at the garments and shake my head. "These are not my clothes."

"Very good, Vi. Next you will be discerning left from right and apples from oranges!" A single eyebrow perks up into a smooth arc. "I would apologize for my sarcasm, but I find myself rather amusing. As for the clothes, they are my mother's. They should fit you. They are older and she has outgrown them."

"But it is a dress..."

He cocks his head to the side, a smirk sidling up his face. "I'm sorry. Did you plan on playing boy at the ball, too? Because I'm afraid it would look awfully odd if I danced with another man. Oh, unless, of course, you wanted me to wear the dress? I always did say red looks marvelous on me. Brings out my eyes." He bats his eyelashes at me and smiles. I sneer, annoyed by his mockery.

"I didn't think your mother was serious. I thought we would simply stay in the cabin. She doesn't honestly want us to go to the ball!"

Laughing, he suspends the hangers on the bathroom door and looks back over his shoulder at me. His eyes travel slowly down my body and back to my face. I pull the robe closer around me. "My mother does not joke. Ever," he says, and laughs again.

The laugh comes from deep within his throat, but does not reach his eyes. He walks back towards me and pauses. "Be a good little girl, Vi, and go back to the bathroom before Gertrude finds out that I have seen you like this and her proper little world falls apart. I have some things I have to do, but I will see you tonight."

I do not answer, his "good little girl" comment itching at me. I brush by him without a word and march back to the bathroom.

"And Vi?" he calls.

Reluctantly, I turn back. He smiles at my scowl and my irritation grows.

"What?" I hiss.

"That grimace will not complement the dress. I do hope you trade it in for that stunning smile of yours. I want you to look beautiful tonight."

"Well, I want you to stick your—" My words are lost in the slam of the cabin door. Adam is gone. It is me and the dress. It is me and my fears. How am I to stay in hiding while attending a ball most likely crawling with Radicals? I sigh.

"At least he gave me gloves," I say to the dress and

carry it back inside the bathroom to get ready for the ball. After all, I want to look stunning for my demise.

—

I look up at Gertrude's reflection in the mirror. She stands behind me, her silver hair pulled back in a slick bun. Gently, she runs a brush through my hair. Her opposite hand trails after the brush, smoothing down the wild curls. The feeling of the brush in my hair soothes my nerves about tonight. I close my eyes, remembering how Mother used to brush my hair every night when I was a little girl.

"I don't know why I bother," she would say. "You'll have every curl in a knot come morning." Then she would go quiet and continue despite her words.

Against my best efforts, tears begin their march down my cheeks. I swipe them away with a quick motion of my hand. A salty blotch develops on the tip of my white glove. I stare at it, hoping Gertrude does not decide this means they are soiled and that I must have a fresh pair. I feel the woman behind me raise her gaze, examining me in the mirror. She frowns.

"Is something wrong, Miss Hamilton?"

I meet her chocolate-brown eyes in the mirror's reflection. "Nothing," I say. "Just nervous about tonight, I suppose."

She nods and continues her brushing. I look at my image in the mirror. The dress Gertrude picked out is a deep red satin. Muted by elegant black-embroidered gauze, the red is stunning without being ostentatious. An open neckline is made even lower with sleeves that fall down around my shoulders. Like the sleeves, the hem of the skirt is beaded and embellished with black lace. The skirt flares out at the bottom, a section of red satin peeking out from beneath the lace. A short train of black lace and gauze trails at the back. Light and airy, the material is perfect for dancing. I look down at the dress fitted to my body and sigh. It is certainly beautiful, just as Adam wanted.

Adam. The very thought of him and the possibilities tonight may hold stir up a storm of fluttering moths around the fire in my heart.

"Gertrude?" I say, a question that has been burning at the back of my mind suddenly pushing its way to my mouth.

"Yes, Miss Hamilton?"

I pause, deciding how best to word what I am about to say. "Did—I mean, where is Adam's—" she shoots me a nasty look at the use of Adam's Christian name and I correct myself instantly. "Sorry. What I meant to say was, where is Mr. Laurence's father?"

She takes a moment to respond and I feel her deciding whether it is her place to give me an answer at all.

"He is with his son," she says finally.

"But Mr. Laurence is—"

She shakes her head. "No. Not Mr. Adam Laurence. His other son."

Dumbfounded, I stare at my furrowed brow and pursed lips in the mirror. If Adam and I are friends as he says, why would he never mention a brother?

"Adam—" Another meaningful glare. "I'm sorry. Mr. Laurence has a brother?"

She nods, never stopping the brush running through my hair. "Mr. Ray Laurence. He is twenty years of age and two years Mr. Adam Laurence's senior."

"Why are they not on the ship, too?" I ask.

At last, the brush stills. Gertrude raises her warm gaze, looking me in the eye. She looks uncomfortable and I can tell she is not as interested in the conversation as I am.

"I should warn you, Miss Hamilton. Mr. Adam Laurence comes from a family that is not very... accepting," she says, not answering my question.

"There is nothing there for you to warn me against, Gertrude. We are friends. That is all." Even as the words leave my mouth, I know they aren't true, and by the way she shifts behind me I am certain she knows, too.

"Of course, Miss Hamilton. I am sorry. It was not my place to get involved."

I smile at her. "No need for apologies, Gertrude."

She bows her head and continues to brush my hair.

We fall back into silence. I puzzle over her message, her warning. What did she mean by the Laurences not being an accepting family? Mrs. Laurence is the most accepting person I have ever met. Adam, on the other hand, does not know the real me and will never learn the truth, so how can he accept what he will never know?

I dismiss her warning and allow myself to get lost in the relaxing rhythm of the brush running through my hair.

It is only later that I realize the truth in my mother's favorite saying:

The maids know everything.

14
DANCING

Smiling brightly, Dela collapses into the chair beside me. She brushes a piece of blonde hair out of her face and pins it back into place atop her head. With a sigh, she leans back, thin fingers gripping her gloves. She pulls them back over her elbows. The fingertips are slightly soiled, and I wonder how long it will take Mrs. Laurence to scold Dela into putting on a fresh pair.

Reaching out my own gloved hand, I grab the stem of my champagne glass. I swirl it around before taking a tiny sip, bubbles wafting up my nose. I sneeze. Dela hands me her handkerchief and smiles.

"Thank you," I say, taking the lacy white cloth.

She tilts her head to meet my eyes, her worried expression making me wary of the talk I am sure follows.

I gaze out over the dance floor, avoiding her cool glare. Couples swirl around one another in a Boston waltz. The floor is a rainbow of colors as girls in their vibrant dresses twirl and spin around their partners.

An orchestra sits atop a raised platform at the front of the ballroom. Thin bows pull against silver strings, their tips biting at the air with every corresponding movement of the musicians' hands. They fall and rise together in time with the velvet flow of the music as notes pour from the violas and violins, and a deeper voice sounds from the cellos and basses. I watch the bows' movement, a beautiful waltz that is all their own.

"Elvira, why are you sitting here, sipping champagne you do not even like and telling men your dance card is full when we both know that is not true? Please, dance. If not for me, then for yourself. You cannot sit here all night. People are already talking," Dela whispers.

I cross my arms stubbornly, never taking my eyes off the orchestra. "Let them talk."

She frowns angrily. "It is not our image you are corrupting, El. We owe Mrs. Laurence our best behavior tonight. We owe everything to her. Please do not mess this up," she pleads. "This is our only chance. The Laurences are our only chance."

I sigh, raising my gaze to look in her icy blue eyes. She is a vision in pink. Her dress: light pink chiffon with jeweled butterflies adorning the sleeves. It is simplistic, yet elegant.

"Why can you not simply be like every other twelve-year-old?" I say, smiling. "You are too wise for your own good, Dela. I hope you know that."

A grin stretches across her face. "And you, my sister, are too stubborn for your own good. Do promise you will dance with the next man who asks."

I nod and reluctantly take another sip of the champagne. I gaze back out over the dance floor and see Mrs. Laurence staring at us from across the room. She smiles, points to Dela, and curls back her index finger in a beckoning motion.

Dela catches my gaze and follows my line of sight. She sighs dramatically.

"I think Mrs. Laurence wishes to speak with you," I say.

She grimaces. "No doubt to complain about my soiled gloves again. This is my third pair. She has made poor Gertrude run back to the room twice already."

"Well, you had better go. She looks persistent."

Dela stands, smoothing out her dress. "Do I look all right? Is my hair a mess?"

"You look beautiful. Now, go. Oh, and your handkerchief," I say, holding the lacy square out.

She wrinkles her nose. "You keep it. I'm sure Gertrude can fetch me another when she goes back for my fourth pair of gloves." Her dress glittering in the light of the crystal chandeliers, Dela turns her back to me and makes her way across the floor to Mrs. Laurence. "Do not forget, El. The first man who asks! No excuses!" she calls over her shoulder, earning a few snide looks from the couples around her. Ladies are not to raise their voices, but Dela is completely unaware.

Laughing, I return my attention to the orchestra as they begin a polka. I pick at a grape on my plate and bite through its succulent skin, juice exploding against my taste buds. It is sour, but serves its purpose of erasing the foul taste of the champagne.

I scan the crowd for the twentieth time, but still there is no sign of him. He was not back at the cabin when we departed for the ball, and although Mrs. Laurence assured us Adam would be meeting us at the dance, he is still absent.

For the hundredth time, I consider leaving the dance in search of him, but with Mrs. Laurence and Gertrude watching me like hawks, there is no chance of sneaking away.

"Miss Hamilton, there you are!" I turn my head to see Gertrude walking up behind me. Speak of the devil, I think, and I fake a smile as she comes to stand before me.

"Good evening, Gertrude. Are you enjoying yourself?" I ask pleasantly.

"Yes. The food is wonderful and the taste in music is exquisite. Mrs. Laurence and I have noticed that you have not been dancing. Are you not feeling well?"

I shake my head. "I feel fine. Why do you ask?"

The lines in her forehead and around her eyes become more prominent as she talks. "Well, some fine young men have asked for a spot on your dance card and you have not danced with one. We thought maybe you were ill. Are you ill?"

I take my time to respond, deciding whether I should lie and claim that I am indeed in poor health, or tell the truth. Remembering my promise to Dela, I decide a slanted version of the truth will suffice.

"I am not ill. I simply am not in the mood to dance," I say slowly, leaving out the part about Adam. The part where I am too busy searching for him to dance. The part where I have no interest in dancing with anyone else, no matter how handsome, wealthy, or chivalrous he may be.

"Well, in that case, Mrs. Laurence would like to see your dance card." She reaches out a hand, palm up, waiting.

The urge to ask why burns in my throat. I reach for the dance card where it hangs from my dress by a hook and ribbon. It is a small leather book with a list of songs the orchestra will be playing throughout the night. A pencil hangs from it, an open invitation for the men of the ball to write their names by the piece of music they wish to dance with me. All twenty-four songs are blank.

I unhook it from my dress and hand it to Gertrude, who smiles and walks away. Within twenty minutes, she returns, hands back the book, and leaves without a word. Unnerved by her mischievous smile, I open the book and groan. Once a blank dance card is now a long list of names, names of men whom I am now forced to accompany on the dance floor.

As if on cue, a gangly boy walks towards me. His hair is a rustic red and his nose too large for his face. His dark tailcoat contrasts his white bow tie. Intermingling with the copper tone of his hair, the winged collar of his shirt seems dreadfully stiff. I must tilt my head all the way back to see him as he is frighteningly tall. He peers at me with dark green eyes. As I stand and we introduce ourselves, I find myself wondering how he can possibly dance with legs so long and lanky.

"Shall I have the pleasure of dancing with you?" he says. His tone is respectful and amicable, and I know that there is no way I can refuse him now.

I stretch a smile and reply, "With pleasure, sir."

With a quick bow, he takes my arm and leads me out onto the dance floor where the other couples have already begun the polka. I place my hand on his shoulder and my other in his palm as he places his free hand against the small of my back.

"Do you know this dance well, Miss Hamilton?" he asks conversationally.

I smile. "Yes. Well enough," I say, and wonder if he can tell I am lying through my teeth. My family was never like these families, the type of families that make frequent calls to their friends and play cricket and attend balls. This is my first ball, my first polka, and my first couple dance, but there is no way I am letting him, or anyone else, know that.

I follow his lead as I put all of my weight onto my left foot and hop onto my right. Together we take three small steps and continue the pattern, moving across the floor with the other couples. I try not to watch my feet as we polka our way from one side of the room to the other. Dela sits in a nearby chair. She captures my eye and winks before I am spinning away from her, completely lost in the music and the steps.

"You have very light feet," the boy, whose name I have already forgotten, remarks. I find his comment odd, but take the compliment with a smile.

As the song ends, we slow and pull apart to clap with the other dancers.

"It was an honor dancing with you, Miss Hamilton," he says, flashing another crooked smile and bowing, his right hand outstretched. I take it and he graciously conducts me to my seat. I sit and smile at him without a word, allowing him to press his lips to my hand. A sigh escapes me as he walks away, but my rest is brief for another man ambles towards me.

The cycle continues for the next six songs as one man after another joins me on the dance floor. I follow their leads, learning the patterns of the steps to each dance as I follow the music across the marble tiles.

When the sixth song ends I excuse myself, claiming I am in need of freshening up, and take my leave. Holding my dress up, I ascend the elegant staircase where I have seen many groups of giggling girls escape in search of the ladies' sitting room.

I turn to my left, where a trio of girls just appeared, and walk down the hall. Carved doors separate the ladies' and men's rooms from all of the others. The sitting room has a mixture of stylish chairs and chaises. A maid who has been assigned to the room offers to help me with my hair, but I decline her proposal. After many more offers, she meanders off to fetch me the fresh pair of gloves I finally agree to. And at last, I am alone.

Looking into one of the many gold encrusted mirrors, I fix my hair, pinning curls back into the elegant twist Gertrude had designed atop my head. A black wisp hangs down to the side of my face and I leave it there, having run out of pins.

I relax into the closest chair, suddenly exhausted, both emotionally and physically. The men I have danced with tonight were indeed fine young men and each one of them showed he was interested. Some more than others, I think, remembering my third partner who kept testing my patience with his wandering hands during the mazurka. But did any of it matter?

Even if I were interested, it couldn't happen. I am Marked. And though, for the time being, I have no powers, the Mark is still a part of me and who I am. Can I truly be with someone who does not really know me? No. This will be my life, dancing with men I can never be with, attending balls and falling for men who will never know the real me.

I want to throw my dance card against the wall. I want to scream at the top of my lungs. I want to share my frustration with the world and the men who thought they had a chance with me. The joke is on them. You can never be with me, and you wouldn't want to be with me if you knew what lies beneath my glove. I laugh maniacally, happy to have the room to myself as I become wild with disappointment.

Giggling through my tears, I wipe at my eyes and clean my face. I shake my head at my reflection, feeling sad for the girl in the mirror who will never be loved.

"No use in feeling sorry for yourself," I tell her. "It is what it is."

It is what it is, I think, remembering Adam's words from the other night: It all depends on the fate of the stars.

And that is life, isn't it? Fate. Luck. Chance. A long series of what-if's that lead from one moment to the next, time never pausing for you to catch your breath, to make sense of the cards that have been handed to you. And all you can do is play your cards and hope for the best, because in the end, it all comes back to those three basics.

Fate. Luck. Chance.

Wanting to escape before the maid returns, I take one more glance at the girl in the mirror and head back to the ball, never anticipating the hand of cards that would be dealt next.

———

15
CHOOSING

From the top of the stairs, the ball appears just as I had always dreamed: girls in beautiful dresses spinning around handsome men to the push and pull of the musicians' bows—music so sweet and powerful implanting a fire in their hearts, driving them across the floor in one ebbing sea of dancers. Only one thing is missing, and that is—

"Adam?"

I lean further over the rail for a better look and sure enough, there he is, and he's not alone. In the middle of the dance floor, he leads a young woman in a Hesitation Waltz. Even from this distance, I can tell she is beautiful. He leans closer to whisper in her ear. She tilts her head back and laughs. My stomach churns. My face grows hot. My heart hammers inside my chest.

Holding my head high, I ignore the feeling in my gut and begin to make my way down the stairs. As much as I try to avoid looking at him, my eyes continue to find a way back. Halfway down the stairs, I pause and sneak a glance. Adam's eyes pass over me, but instantly draw back as he comes to a full stop in the middle of the floor. Wide green eyes stare in my direction; I peer over my shoulder, certain he cannot be staring at me, but there is no one else nearby.

Blushing, I continue my descent down the stairs, never taking my eyes off him. The girl stares at him as if he is crazy, befuddled as to why they stopped. Angry couples glare in his direction, mumbling nasty comments under their breath as they dance around the rude man still standing in the middle of the floor. Adam murmurs something to the girl beside him before making his way through the dancers alone. He heads in my direction and I watch from the third step, my heart picking up tempo.

At last he reaches the staircase. His fiery green eyes stare up at me, his lips slightly parted. He wears expensive black tails and a waistcoat of a lighter color. His trousers are streamlined and fitted. A pristine, white bow tie brushes against the hollow of his neck. Unlike the rest of the men, his dark brown hair is tousled, not smoothed back. He reaches out a hand, never taking his eyes off of me, and I take it.

"I was right," he says, pressing his lips to my hand. My cheeks flare pink and I suddenly wish my glove was not there to separate his lips from my skin.

I smile. "Right about what?"

"You are beautiful." He coughs awkwardly, and then shrugs. "Without the scowl, I mean."

Descending the last three steps, I make sure to scowl at him and stick out my tongue. He laughs.

"Where were you earlier? You never met us back at the cabin. I was afraid you would not show."

"I—"

"There you are! I cannot believe you left me stranded in the middle of the dance floor!" Coming up behind him is the girl he was dancing with only a minute ago. She wraps an arm around his waist and smiles at me. "Oh, hello. And who might you be?"

Before I can respond, Adam clears his throat. "Miss Clara Lindell, may I present Miss Elvira Hamilton," he says, sweeping a hand behind my back. One look into the hidden depths of her baby blues and my decision is clear: I do not like her. I do not like her one bit.

"Pleasure to make your acquaintance," I say, and dip into a slight curtsy.

"No, the pleasure is all mine," she says and turns to Adam. "Is she why you left me during our dance, Adam? Though I can obviously see why." She smiles at me and I smile tightly in turn "You do owe me a dance."

And though I try to ignore her wandering hands and the casual way in which she touches him, a green fury burrows in my chest. She called him Adam, I think. She called him Adam!

137

"Yes, of course. Save me a place on your dance card. I will find you shortly," he answers.

She nods and turns away, but instantly turns back and whispers in his ear, just loud enough for me to hear, "I hope you do not put me off like this when we are married." She grins at me. "Pleasure meeting you," she says, and strolls away. Her hips sway as she moves, blonde waves bouncing atop her head. As much as I want to deny it, she is gorgeous.

Dumbfounded, I stare at Adam. He closes his eyes and bows his head, and I am sure he knows I heard.

"Would you please excuse me? I need some air" I whisper and push past him towards the double doors that lead out onto the deck. I shove my way through groups of men and women engaged in boisterous conversations until I am finally at the doors. I hear him calling my name, but do not stop.

Tasting of salt, the cool night air hits me in one immense wave. Everything grows suddenly hushed. The voices and music of the ball are only a quiet murmur behind the roar of the ocean and the sigh of the wind.

I run to the rail, a silver streak in the night, and lean over. The metal is cold against my skin. It clears my mind for a short moment, before I hear his voice and everything floods back.

"Elvira, wait! Vi!"

He stops calling. Without turning, I know he stands

behind me. I do not move.

We stand there, neither talking, allowing the breeze to rush over our faces and sting our cheeks in silence. He steps forward, hesitantly, until he is at the rail.

"You are engaged," I whisper. It is more a statement than a question.

He grabs my wrist, making me turn around. I do so reluctantly. His eyes burn into my own, pleading and apologizing all at once. However, I do not wish for his sympathy. I wish to be alone. I wish for him to leave so that I may cry in peace. Neither wish comes true. He stays, holding onto me with nothing but his eyes.

"I am not engaged," he says at last.

"Oh?" I choke out.

He moves closer. "Clara's family and my family have been close friends for years. Our marriage was determined before either of us was even born."

I look him in the eye. "So you are to be married to her?"

He nods. "I am supposed to propose."

"But you haven't," I whisper.

"No. No, I have not."

A dim light of hope appears before my rationale instantly blacks it out. "But you will propose, won't you?"

He shrugs, turning back to the ocean. The moonlight and stars dance across the water. The sky surrounds us. It has no end. No reason. No secrets. It has only the dance.

"My life has always been mapped out for me. I was always like this ship, never wandering from the planned course. And then, one day, I took a step away from the intended path to help a girl." He turns his head. His eyes lock with mine in a meaningful glance. "I never questioned my intended marriage to Clara. It was my future. My only future. And I never questioned it."

"But you are questioning it now?" My chest tightens. Every molecule of air halts within my body, waiting for his answer, needing to know if all hope is truly lost.

Another shrug. "Things have changed. I have changed."

"Things could not have changed so much as to make you question your proposal, though," I say. I scold myself, unsure as to why I am defending his marriage to another woman.

"The slightest change often yields the greatest consequence," he responds.

The truth of his words resonates inside my heart. After all, a Marked man started a war with a single murder. A tiny Mark became the difference between predator and prey. And one terrible night changed two lives forever.

There is no denying it. It is a testament stamped in years of history, and history does not lie. Adam's path was all before him, clear and smooth, with no other choices branching out. But circumstances change. Small causes lead to large effects. New paths are added.

And all anyone can do is choose.

I peer out into the distance. A never-ending ocean. A never-ending sky. Any direction is a possibility for the ship, but there is only one path for me. Forward. And whether forward moves me closer or further away from him does not matter. All that matters is that I go.

Adam turns to me. Blazing green eyes yell out, trying to tell me something, but the message is lost to their fiery depths. "Elvira, I—"

I'll never know what he was about to say; a high scream pierces the air before he can finish. Our attention snaps back to the ball. Another cry, then another and another. People stampede back and forth before the ballroom's French doors. The doors fly open. A rush of women and men charge out onto the deck. They push and shove, not caring who lies at the other end of their panicky hands. There is only one goal: to escape.

My first thought is of Dela. I search the faces that spill out of the doors, but my sister is absent. I scan over the deck, wondering if she already got out and knowing in my gut that she didn't. No. She is still inside. My head fills with thoughts of the Radicals and I wonder if that is what this is all about. Did they find her? Was Dela discovered?

Blood rushes to my brain, making me dizzy as my heart thumps, faster and faster, against my chest. I suck in air with shallow breaths as the sudden events unfold. I look to Adam as though he might know what is happening, as though this is something that often happens at balls. But his expression instantly shuts down any daft hope I might have possessed.

He stares in shock, his mouth agape and his eyes wide, as if in disbelief that anything like this could happen in his perfect little world. As for me, I am all too familiar with the frightened faces and deafening screams. It is the very essence of war. The Marked's war. My war.

His light eyes find mine, his pupils so small they are almost lost to the green. Too much white frames his irises. He is scared, I realize. Cocky, composed Adam is scared. I step forward, but he catches my arm. He shakes his head, his face wild. I look down at his hand wrapped around my wrist. In the back of my mind, I register its pale coloring. It does not stop me, however. I gaze up at him and offer a weak smile before wrenching my arm out of his grasp and racing towards the ballroom.

I push my way against the endless flow of people streaming from the doors. A man falls against me, knocking me down. He lies on top of me, and I push at him until finally he crawls away with the rest of the crowd. I try to get to my feet, but people rush over me, kicking me back down with every attempt I make at standing.

A hand reaches down, plucking me out of the stampede. Suddenly, my feet are under me. I turn around, and Adam stares at me with a little smile and shrugs. I smile back, relieved in knowing I am not alone. A woman knocks against me, and I fall back into his arms. A cacophony of panicked voices mixes with the beat of his heart. He pulls me up onto my feet again. With Adam at my back, I push forward through the throng until at last we drop onto the marble floor of the ballroom, the horde of people at our backs.

On all fours, I fight to regain my breath. Raising my gaze, I throw my head back to keep the black curls that had escaped their pins from obscuring my eyesight. Another rush of people runs towards me, accompanied by a storm of shrieks and hollers. I freeze. My mind tells me to move, but I am trapped in the path of the door. I watch as dozens of feet bear down on me. I squeeze my eyes shut, bracing for the pain, when Adam's iron grip surrounds my waist.

He pulls me to the side just as the first person slams down on the exact spot where I had been kneeling. I release a sigh and lean back into him. His breathing is loud in my ear. I peel my gaze away from the people charging for the doors and redirect it towards the mayhem unfolding in the ballroom.

With the number of people who ran out onto the deck, I expect the room to be nearly empty. But I am wrong. People are everywhere. Men. Women. Children. First-class passengers mix with butlers and waiters. In the chaos, the world's classes have melded together to form a new class that can only be described as crazed.

I peer over their heads in search of the cause. Adam squeezes my shoulder, nodding towards the doors where

Gertrude and Mrs. Laurence have appeared. They wave at us, trying earnestly to draw us outside. I nod for him to leave. He hesitates for a moment, grabbing my hand and giving it a gentle squeeze, before jogging over to his mother. I do not move. Not until I find Dela.

Five men rush past in pursuit of a mother and her three children. The little ones grip her hands, tiny fingers clinging desperately to their solace, to the one person who might save them. As the woman readjusts her grip on the smallest child, I catch a glimpse of her arm. I gasp, not believing it to be true in my heart, but knowing in my head that what I see is real. A green Crescent consumes the inside of her left wrist.

This woman, these children—they are Marked.

They are Marked and they are hunted.

I shiver, watching helplessly as the men chase the terrified family towards the kitchens. Lifting the smallest child up onto her back, the mother continues forward. I move closer, needing to know what happens next, needing to know if perchance death is not the Marked's only option. If this family can escape then maybe there is hope for Dela and me yet!

Pushing my way through the crowd, I follow the Radicals across the ballroom as everyone else flees in the opposite direction. A man steps in my path, obscuring my vision and knocking me down. He steps over me and continues his escape, thinking nothing of the girl still lying on the floor.

Feet smack down around me. I begin to crawl, weaving in and out of the crowd towards an upturned table. The tablecloth drapes over one of the legs that jut out in midair. Hidden beneath its cover, I look out over the floor in search of the Radicals. At last, I spot them, standing just outside the kitchen doors.

The Marked woman and her children are nowhere in sight.

I smile, thinking they have gotten away before I hear, "They locked themselves inside. What do you want us to do?"

The man addressed strokes his chin, glancing back and forth between the small window in the kitchen door and his men. "Let's—"

"Sir!" A younger man yells. His wide gaze fixates on the window, his nose pressing against the glass. "The woman is starting a fire!"

I cover my mouth to keep from making a sound as this new information seeps in. Why would she do such a thing? It was suicide!

Suicide. I stare in horror.

The leading Radical whirls on the door and pushes the younger man aside. He looks through the glass, a smirk sidling up his face. Turning on his men, he begins to laugh. A booming, guttural laugh that bubbles out from deep within him. They all join in until their mirth almost drowns out the distant cries. Almost.

"Leave them there. They'll be dead in a few minutes," the man tells his colleagues. All four of them nod in agreement, still laughing at the ease in which they disposed of the Marked family. "Come along. Mr. Simmons said he saw two leeches take off up the stairs."

As soon as they are out of sight, I rush for the doors. A thick smoke swirls on the opposite side of the glass and seeps out from underneath the door. Through its haze, I see the mother starting another fire with the stove. The three children sit on the floor, crying. Another figure, one I had not seen with the Marked woman before, bangs at the door, yelling incoherently. I squint, trying to see through the smog when the figure steps back and I meet the familiar light blue of her eyes.

"Dela?"

16
LIVING

Every muscle tightens. Every breath of air halts. Desperation seizes me, a plume of fire growing at the pit of my stomach. It spreads up through my arms and down through my legs. It burns at the tips of my fingers and toes. It burns brighter than the flaying flames behind my sister.

This fire, this energy, surges up inside of me until I have no choice but to release. With no warning, I run forward, slamming my body against the door and screaming at the top of my lungs. I bang my fists against the wood. Incoherent words jumble together into one desperate howl.

"Dela!" I scream. "Let her out! Let her out! Dela!"

Relentlessly, I pound at the door. My face wears a salty sheen of tears and sweat. Black curls have escaped Gertrude's beautiful twist. They stick to my jaw and fly around my face as I shake my head from side to side.

"Open the door! Dela, open the door! Please! Dela!"

She cries on the other side, her tiny hands smacking against the door in rhythm with my own. "She thought I was alone, El! She thought I was alone and told me she had a better place for us to go!" she yells. The words are muffled by the door and the cries of the disturbed night. "I don't want to go with her, El. I don't want to go. Please, don't make me go." Her cries are hysterical now. She can scarcely get the words out between each shuddering breath and racking sob.

"You don't have to go, Dela. You don't have to," I cry. "Just open the door!"

She shakes her head wildly. "I can't! She—she is keeping it locked with her mind," she blubbers. "She's like Mother. She can do things," another fearful whimper bubbles out, "with her mind."

A Kinetic? A thousand thoughts whip through my mind. I need help. Dela! There's not much time. Dela! I need a plan. Dela! She will die! Get her out! Dela! Dela! Dela!

"It's so hot, El." She leans against the door. I can see her gasping for breath as her lungs battle the ash and smoke.

"Stay close to the floor, Dela. I will not leave you!" I yell. "I will get you out! I promise!"

I search the room, looking for anyone who might help me. Only a few scattered persons still walk the ballroom.

"Dela! Are you still there?"

"I'm here, El. I'm still here." Her voice is faint. Fear

threatens to overtake me.

I bite back my tears, not wanting to scare her. "Can you sing a song to me, Dela? Can you sing a song for me?"

She does not answer, but before long her quiet voice begins to carry through the door. "Rockaby, lullaby, bees in the clover..."

My heart contracts in adoration for my sister as she croons the song I sang to help her sleep. I look past Dela at the Marked woman. She sits on the floor with the children, holding them tight. She thinks she is doing the right thing, that this will save them. She thinks this is a way out! But she is wrong. Death is no escape.

The Marked woman can take her life and the lives of her children, but she cannot take the life of my sister!

"Keep singing, Dela!" I yell as I search the room for help.

Two women stumble towards the doors, crying and moaning. A young girl lies on her back near an upturned chair. I cannot see her face, but I fear the worst. Neither of the two are any help to me. Then I see him. A man most likely in his mid-thirties running for the stairs.

"Sir!" I yell, following after him. He does not stop. "Sir! Please! I need your help!"

He hesitates on the second step and that is all I need. I grab onto his hand. He tries to rip it free and leave behind the frantic girl clinging to his arm, but I hold on tight.

"Let me go, child," he says. His voice is deep, much

deeper than I would have thought. Fear grows inside of me at the warning in his tone.

"Please. My sister—she is locked in the kitchen—she—"

The man jerks his hand back hard and I fall forward. My forearm smacks against a step. It throbs dully, but it is nothing compared to the pain of knowing I am running out of time.

Turning around, he continues his ascent up the stairs.

"You coward! She will die!" I shriek. "She will die! You must help me! She will die!"

Lost in my fury, my pleads verge upon hysterical. My whole being becomes crazed as I hammer my fists against the marble step, needing a release. Within seconds, I am trembling like someone who has just escaped an insane asylum.

I am blinded by my tears and do not see the hands that abruptly wrench me to my feet.

The man's voice is close to my ear as he says, "Do not make me regret this. I cannot Hold it for long, so explain quickly."

I open my eyes and blink away the tears, until through the glassy haze, I meet the long lashes that frame his swimming black orbs.

"Hold wha—" I begin, but the answer stuns me into silence.

My world has frozen over.

Mouths hang open—the screams, the sounds, stopped

in time. The silence is deafening. Nothing moves. People stand in their huddled groups, but they do not hold each other for comfort. They do not rub each other's backs like Mother used to rub mine whenever a bad dream left me in a cold sweat. No, these people are motionless, still, immobile. They are lost in an infinite moment in time.

The moment drags forward. No one cries. Voices are caught in the air. If I look at the refugees' open mouths long enough, I can almost imagine the noises that would have been. But my imaginings are not reality. No. The real thing is lost, vanished to this new silent world where everyone—everything—has paused.

Everything except us.

I open my mouth to speak, to ask one of the numerous questions that vie for the starting jump off my tongue, but the man beats me to it.

"It would seem we are not so different," he states gruffly.

Instantly, I know what he speaks of and involuntarily make a move for my left wrist. He nods, a condescending smile playing across his lips.

"That's right, child," he says.

I shake my head. "But how could you have known?"

He smiles. "Two days ago I saw those same violet eyes beneath a bowler. Now, the same eyes come to me pleading for help. Only one thing would drive a young girl to dress as a boy and sneak onto a ship in these dark times." He pauses. "So, what are you? A Kinetic? Truth-Seeker? Mediator, perhaps?"

I shake my head. "I—I don't know. My powers have not exactly—"

Before I can finish, he jerks my left arm forward and peels back my glove. His face is meant to be neutral, but I see the subtle shift in his eyes as he takes in my Mark. He grunts.

"I am losing the Hold," he says, his voice strained. "Just explain what happened. Quickly."

"My sister is caught in the kitchens with another Marked woman and her children. The woman has started a fire. I think—I think she means to commit suicide. Please. You must help me get her out!" I start out calm, but by the end of my explanation, I am blubbering like a fool. "She will die. We haven't much time!"

He surprises me with a laugh. "There is always enough time in my world," he utters, throwing in a wink for good measure.

I scowl, ready to scream at him, to tell him that this is no time for winks and laughter, but before I can so much as open my mouth, the Hold breaks.

The silence ends. The world floods back to life.

However, it is not the sudden motion that startles me, but the onslaught of noise. Rising and swelling, the abrupt sounds of the disturbed night hit me like a ton of bricks. The refugees' voices pound in my ears. They join together into one thunderous harmony that makes me lightheaded. I reach out a hand and grab the man's shoulder to steady myself.

"You get used to it after a while," he says as he takes in my wobbly feet and the trembling hands cupped over my ears. "Keep close now, child." My thoughts flash back to the night that started it all. Mother's sweet whisper that urged us to keep close as we raced down our house's worn steps for the last time. The memory steals the breath from my body, but somehow my feet manage to stay in the present, following after the man at a run as my mind still wallows in the past.

I snap back to attention as we come to an abrupt stop before the kitchen doors. Racing towards the little window, I peer through the glass. Four bodies slump to the floor before the stove. The Marked woman's arms wrapped around the three young children even in death. The little hands held tightly in her own. Their faces are relaxed, as though they have fallen into a pleasant sleep, but I know the truth. I know about the inhaled smoke, the true reason for the Marked family's closed eyes.

I know how it ended for this desperate family.

I know why.

And I know who is at fault.

But the one truth that burns brightest in my mind is that a fourth Marked child is missing. My sister. Wild violet eyes scan over the kitchen, but I do not see her. For a moment, the hope that maybe she had escaped on her own blooms inside of me.

Until I see the feet, jutting out from a tiny crumpled body that I know lies just against the door. Only her legs and feet are visible from this awkward angle through the window, but I recognize the pink chiffon and silk slippers. I recognize the pale white feet that used to run out of the house barefoot into my garden, Mother's shouts following them out the door, insisting the young girl put on a pair of shoes. I see the mischievous smile that would light the young girl's face as she ignored Mother's calls and sat down beside me.

"What kind of flowers are these?" she would ask.

And I would smile, always happy to share my knowledge of gardening with anyone who would listen. Dela was an excellent listener. She would nod and smile and ask questions, until, at last, Mother would stomp out of the house and insist Dela come back inside.

"But Mother," she would say, "I want to live."

And my mother would look at her dubiously and say, "What do you mean, dear? You are living."

Then Dela would giggle and shake her head as though she understood a joke we could not possibly comprehend. "No, Mother. I want to live. I want to feel the mud squish between my toes and run through the grass to the beach and feel the cold water against my bare feet. That is living. Wearing uncomfortable shoes while being polite to people you do not even like at afternoon tea? Never playing? That is not living, Mother. That is not living."

And not for the first time, I was taken aback by my sister's strange maturity.

Mother would scoff, grab Dela by the arm, and usher her to the house as she said, "If I ever hear you talking like that again, you will get a bar of soap in that dirty mouth of yours, do you hear me? We do not speak like that. Young ladies do not speak like that!"

I always idolized my sister for that trait, for her willingness to dance along the line between what is proper and what is not.

I want to live.

Those four words echo in my mind as I stare at the crumpled body of my sister. My sister, who only ever wanted to truly live. My sister, who I had promised I would bring to America safely. A promise I am not about to break now.

17
BREATHING

My arms quiver with the task of holding the unwieldy object above my head. I believe it is a part of a door that had broken from its hinges during the chaos, but I cannot be sure. Standing behind the Marked man, I hold the back end of the wooden fragment as he supports the front.

"On the count of three, then," he yells back to me.

I begin to tell him that counting is a waste of time, but he has already begun spouting out the numbers.

"One."

I readjust my hold.

"Two."

I plant my feet.

"Three!"

I yell with the effort as I drive the splintered door forward into the window. The glass shatters, showering down upon the floor, creating a carpet of deadly beauty. Without wasting any time, the Marked man reaches a hand through the now open square, carefully avoiding the few shards still clinging to the frame. Smoke drifts out into the ballroom, making us cough and wheeze. His hand fumbles along the inside of the door, until at last, I hear a click and the door swings outward.

"The Marked woman's Hold over the lock has broken. She must already be dead," he remarks, but I do not listen.

I scrabble forward into the room, holding my breath partly because of the smoke and partly because I am terrified it may already be too late. Lying directly in the middle of the doorway is my sister. A solitary whimper escapes my lips. Slender white fingers clutch the sleeve of pale pink to Dela's mouth. It is as though the world has frozen once again for I cannot move. I can only stare at the horror that is my fallen sister.

The Marked man steps in front of me, pushing me out of the way as he reaches under Dela's arms and drags her out of the increasing smoke. I redirect my gaze at him in jealous wonder. She is my sister and yet, what did I do? I stared. I did not move. I did not help. I simply watched as this man, who I have only known for a few short moments, pulled her out of harm's way. Shame and guilt tear into my heart.

"She's not breathing," the man mumbles under his breath. As if to match his statement, I stop breathing as well.

Not breathing? Not breathing! My mind fumbles

over those two simple words. Not breathing means death. Not breathing means I have lost my sister. Not breathing means I have failed. I cannot—no, will not—accept those words. She is alive. She will breathe. She is alive! I think again and again, willing it to be true.

The man tilts her head back and opens her mouth. I begin to ask what he is doing when his actions stun me into silence. Bending forward, he presses his mouth over Dela's. Anger boils inside of me and I run forward to knock him away from her when I see something I never thought I'd see again. Her chest rises. I pause, entranced by this Marked man. In a daze of hope and fascination, I watch in silence as he breathes air into my sister.

He breathes. Her chest rises. He breathes. Her chest rises. The pattern repeats until he suddenly wrenches back.

"No!" I scream. "You cannot stop now! She was breathing! You were helping her breathe! Keep going! You mustn't stop! You mustn't give up!"

"Be calm, child. Be calm and look." He nods his head towards my sister, still lying on the ground. I do as he says and look until I cannot look anymore. Her body, so still and motionless, wrangles out a cry from deep within me and I collapse to my knees. I move closer. My hands tremble over her smooth face. They fumble over her closed lids, over her silken blonde lashes and hair.

I rest my head against her chest as a torrent of tears

slides over the bridge of my nose and down my cheek, creating a salty splotch on her sweet dress and forming a glossy sheen on the shelf of my upper lip. Choked sobs scratch through my throat and bubbles form around my mouth. I look terrible. I look as though my entire world has fallen apart, as though my reason for existence has died. And perhaps it is true.

Burying my face into her chest, I squeeze my eyes shut against the pain. My cheek moves in rhythm with her chest as she breathes.

As she breathes?

Jerking back, I stare intently at my sister, waiting for hope to shine through, knowing that hope will find its way to me again in the form of her rising chest. The short moment it takes for her chest to lift again feels as if it is an eternity, but at last, it happens. Again and again, she breathes. My sister breathes! A contagious joy pulses in my blood. It makes me want to touch her, to wrap her in my arms, to hold her closer than humanly possible, and to never let go.

I emit an odd noise somewhere between a whimper and a sigh, pressing my face into her hair and planting a kiss on her cheek.

"Dela," I whisper. "Everything will be all right, my sister. You are safe now. I am here."

I turn to the Marked man. He sits back on his haunches, watching my sister and me. His lip quirks up, almost becoming a smile.

"You saved her," I say. "You helped her breathe!" Overcome with emotion, I throw my arms around this man I hardly even know and hold him tight. "Thank you," I murmur into his shoulder. Though I expect him to shrink away, he surprises me by patting my back in an attempt to comfort.

"She is awakening," he says into my ear and I release him, whirling on my sister. Dela's light pools of blue blink open, falling upon me. Veins of red trace around the white of her eyes. Her once-blue lips begin to slowly regain their color. She smiles and I smile back.

"El?" she chokes out.

"Dela!" I shriek with elation. With one step forward, I am embracing my sister and she is holding me with weak arms.

"The Marked family?" she whispers.

I cannot help looking back at the door, still slightly ajar. Through the black haze, I can just see a tiny unmoving hand. I shake my head. Dela's bottom lip trembles as she tries to fight back the tears.

"It is all right, Dela. You are safe and that is all that matters."

"But th-those children..."

I shush her, rubbing her back and stroking her hair. "They are in a happier place now, Dela."

"No!" she screams, her voice raw. She pushes away

from me and stands in a sudden surge of rage. Startled by her abrupt strength, I pull back. "You sound just like her—like that Marked woman! It is horrible! She was wrong and so are you!"

Dela's outburst is too much for her and a fit of coughing consumes her body.

"I'm sorry, Dela. Please forgive me. You are right and I should not have said it."

The Marked man clears his throat and we both whirl on him. "If I may, I do believe there is still a ship in chaos. Pardon my suggestion, but perhaps this conversation is better saved for a later time."

"Who is he?" Dela asks, staring at the man suspiciously.

"This is..." With a surge of bewilderment, I realize I do not know. I held this man by the hand as I begged for his help and yet, I did not know his name. He breathed life back into my sister and yet, I did not know is name. It feels odd, looking back on it now, that I could ask so much of a man and still not ask something as simple as a name.

"Mack Eversby," he answers for me.

"Yes. Mr. Eversby—"

"—saved your dear life," he finishes with a smirk.

Dela starts. "I am much obliged to you, then, Mr. Eversby."

He laughs. "No one owes me, and likewise, I owe no one. That is how I prefer it. Now, both of you, follow me."

Dela immediately starts after him, but I cannot

move. I stare around at the now-empty ballroom and at the double doors that wave back and forth in the night as though in farewell to those fallen. Beyond the doors, the screams and yells become one with the howl of the wind. I know that I should run. I should flee with Mr. Eversby and Dela while I still can, but something pulls me back, something makes me gravitate closer to the doors and further away from my Marked companions. No, not something. Someone.

Adam.

18
SAVING

I used to think I knew everything about the Marked's war. After all, I had seen it firsthand—the pain, the loss, the blood. I watched men fall beneath the blows of fellow men. I watched a woman take her own life to escape the agony and suffering, her children dying senselessly alongside her. I knew the look in the prey's eyes—that moment when he realizes his life is over. I knew it all.

Or so I thought.

As I gaze out across the deck, I find the one thing I did not know before, the one thing I was too childish and self-centered to see. This war does not only affect the Marked and the Radicals—it affects everyone. Another group exists, caught between these two warring factions. Tears line pathways down to their hearts, gliding over parted lips that cry out into the night. Ordinary people. Normal people. Innocent people.

People who feel the prodding of the war's gun just as much as we. Large groups, small groups—all huddled together as though, by squeezing in tightly enough, nothing bad can pervade their circle. But in truth, the war will touch them, just as it will touch all of us. And the tighter they squeeze together, the harder the enemy will try to break them apart. But who is the enemy of these bystanders?

Not us. Not them. Only the work of fate. For it is fate that has brought this tragedy upon them.

I look into the faces—the eyes hiding behind films of tears. This is a whole new world to them. They send their husbands and their sons out into this world. They hear the stories and cluck their tongues in sympathy, but they do not understand this world. They think they do, but no one truly understands until they live it, until they see this world firsthand. This world of war.

Pushing my way through the crowd, skimming over the faces in search of Adam, I see the understanding in their eyes. There is no denying that they understand now. Fear radiates from their every fiber. Terror twines into their bones. Yes, they understand now and I almost pity them. I almost wish the war had not popped their bubble of safety and comfort, that the war had not ruined this peaceful night, but at least they understand now. At least, they understand.

"Everyone! Everyone, please, lend me your attention!"

A deep commanding voice cuts through the crowd. My head snaps up along with a hundred others. A man stands on a bench, looking down over the passengers of the ship as he waits for silence. Every mouth shuts. The sudden quiet has a haunting quality and I fidget with nervousness.

"I, Benjamin Gleadell, as Captain of the RMS *Celtic*, would like to offer my most severe apology. The Contingents were given strict orders about their search for the Marked. I can assure you, the rest of your trip will be one of peace and comfort. Please excuse their actions and return to your cabins for the night. Enjoy the rest of your evening!"

I glance at the men and women standing around me, attempting to gauge their reactions as my own anger threatens to spill over. Lives were lost! The Contingency is a lavish name for the Radicals, for the murderers who just attacked innocent passengers! And the Captain wishes us all a good night? He sends us off to bed as though the past twenty minutes were simply a nightmare?

I watched a woman and her children die.

I nearly lost my sister.

But I am supposed to pretend it never happened. I am supposed to return to my cabin, curl into bed, and forget this terrible night ever occurred. I am supposed to enjoy the rest of my evening as images of smoke and little white hands haunt my dreams.

My blood churns with rage. Angry tears well in my eyes and my fingernails dig into the palms of my hands, forming miniature crescent moons. The back of my throat aches with the irate words I yearn to scream.

All around me feet shuffle and arms bump against arms as people disappear back to their bubbles of comfort and safety. They return to their cabins, the world of war shut away inside a smoke-filled kitchen, visible only through a small window. The passengers had their peek and now they walk away, as if the four slumped bodies still lying on the floor are nothing but the imaginings of a nightmare.

They can erase the nightmare from their minds, but it will weigh down their hearts for all eternity. It was real. For if it wasn't real, am I? Do I exist in a world where the Marked and the Radicals and war are just figments of imagination? Does blood not run through my veins just as it runs through theirs? Do I not matter? Can I be erased, forgotten? Was I ever even known?

Not in their world.

Not in a world where the veracity of war is tucked away into closed hearts and the lips that murmur against teacups are too afraid to speak up.

Unable to submit to denial, I hold my place among the flowing crowd. Somewhere, a child is crying. The mother shushes the young boy and lifts him into her arms.

"It is all right, dear," she murmurs against his thick blond hair. "It is all over."

I watch from where I stand as the woman strokes his

cheek and pats his head. She hands him a small toy. A smile lights his grim face. With the child calmed at last, the mother pushes past me towards the cabins. I move out of her way and watch her passage through the crowd.

A man knocks against her arm, making the little boy drop his toy. His high-pitched screams fill the night and the woman hurriedly bends down to retrieve the plaything. The man reaches for the toy, as well, but he suddenly pauses.

I take a step closer, unsure of why they both stopped. A sudden fear gleams in the mother's eyes. I move nearer and follow the man's gaze. He is fixated on the woman's wrist where her glove, far too big for her thin arms, has gathered at the top of her wrist. Her whole body becomes rigid as her gaze rises to meet his, but he is too busy staring at her arm, at the Mark. Brown, almost black, against her skin, it is impossible to miss.

Please. I see the word form on her lips. Her eyes plead with the man, but with an apology weighing down his gaze, he snaps back up to his full height and yells, "Here! A Marked! Seize her!"

With only a few words, the deck breaks into sheer chaos. A horde closes in around the woman and small boy. Caught in the middle, I fight to keep standing as angry men push against me. They push closer, collapsing in on the small parcel of deck where the family just stood. I cannot see them anymore.

Fear and fury rip through my core, fueling my mind and heart. My adrenaline rushes with these mixed emotions and before I know it, I am squirming my way to the center of it all. The people around me swivel their heads, craning their necks to see even as they walk away. But some are not even capable of walking away. They remind me of moths flitting around the flickering flame of a candlestick in the blackest night. Unable to turn away, they crowd around the very thing they should avoid. The rush, the excitement, the risk of dancing near the burning flames only draws them closer.

I trip over someone lying on the ground and a hand grasps my leg as a man tries to claw his way back to his feet. Fingernails rake against my skin. I kick ferociously until my foot connects with something solid. I try not to think about it as I shove by two more men, spit flying from their mouths as they cry for murder and justice—two words I did not believe could go together.

At last, I make it to the heaviest concentration of people. They stand in a circle, creating a barrier around the events unfolding in the center. I hear the little boy shrieking, and although it is like icicles piercing my heart, a small joy accompanies the fear. Like a newborn baby, crying means life, and for that I am happy.

With shoulders butting up against shoulders, the circle is like a concrete wall, separating me from the little boy. I punch at their backs, trying to squeeze by, but they are too engrossed in the scene to notice. Infuriated by my inability to make it through, I back up. Squeezing my eyes shut, I lunge for the spot where the men's shoulders meet. The hard blockade breaks and suddenly, I am falling, my eyes still clamped shut. I crash against the deck, groaning as sharp needles rip through my shoulder.

I open my eyes. Obscured at first by its proximity, I cannot process what I am seeing until I move my head back. The realization slams into my stomach with full force. Brown eyes, filmed over with death, stare vacantly back at me. Blood spittle trails from parted lips, trickling down over the neck and staining the deck crimson.

They killed her. I was too late and they killed her.

Her boy's cries create a constant background of anguish and sorrow. He stands over his mother's body, screaming and staring. His hands clasp together, shaking as his body racks with sobs. I peer up at him, my sympathy not making either of us feel any better.

Too focused on these figures, I do not notice the three Radicals standing around me and the crowd just beyond them. That is, until a warm liquid falls onto my cheek. Rain? I brush a hand over it and bring my hand down in front of my face. A red smear paints my palm. Confused, I glance up.

In the hand of a Radical gleams the silver edge of a knife, already slick with blood. As if in slow motion, I watch as another red bead falls onto my brow. I blink, wiping above my eye in disgust. My gut wrenches. This is her blood.

The man with the knife glares down at me in repulsion. "You better leave, girl. Or else my blade will find its way into your gut next."

I shiver. With unbelievable speed, his fingers suddenly wind into my hair, lifting me to my feet. I cry out, but the cheering of the crowd overcomes my sole voice. He thrusts me to the edge of the circle and I fall back against the men standing there. They push me away. I stumble, still standing on the periphery of the circle.

The knife-wielding man steps towards the little boy, but another Radical grabs his arm. His eyes flaring with ire, the man glowers at the hand gripping his forearm.

"What are you doing?" he growls.

The younger Radical holding his arm shifts with nervousness, but his blue eyes glint with self-assurance. "He is only a child, Father. He is harmless."

An all-knowing snicker rises in the father's throat. "And what do you think happens to harmless children like him, son? I'll tell you. The bastards grow up to be just like their leech parents! I let him live and he is one more Marked defiling the human race with his black blood. We must spill that blood now!"

As he yells this last statement, he breaks out of his son's grip, charging for the still sobbing boy. Without a single thought, my feet are moving beneath me, carrying me forward. The knife rises in the air, ready to strike, but as it lowers, my hand clamps around the little boy's wrist, jerking him towards me. The Radical lashes at empty air, befuddled for only a slight moment before his wild gaze settles on me.

"You!" he spits. "I warned you, girl!"

The seed of terror implanted with my first step forward starts to blossom. It sprouts vines that slither like snakes into my chest, constricting my heart, forcing it to pump faster and faster. They make their way into my hands, causing them to quiver, and continue down to my feet, rooting me in place. The vines gag my vocal cords; I cannot speak. Bile rises, sour against my tongue.

The fear blooms within me until my whole body feels its effects. Somehow my trembling hands manage to push the child behind me.

"Hand him over and maybe I'll let you live," the Radical says.

Still unable to find my voice, I shake my head. I feel the crowd's intake of breath, their cheers suddenly gone and replaced with silence.

He smirks. "Wrong answer, my dear."

He pulls the knife back, readying for the blow. I close my eyes and stand erect, tensing for the pain...

This is it. I am going to die.

But it never comes. A flurry of movement to my left raises a gust of air. My eyes snap open just in time to see a man plowing into the Radical. They both collapse to the deck, but with no delay are back on their feet. The Radical faces me, but the other man blocks his path. Yelling incoherently, the Radical lunges for the man. Just barely escaping the sharp point of the knife, the other man jerks to his left. The Radical's back is now to me, but he does not want me anymore. He wants the man who tried to stop him. He wants the man who now faces me, blazing green eyes burning with intensity.

He wants Adam.

Pure, cold panic floods through me, freezing the vines of fear where they stand. I cannot breathe, only watch in horror. My grip around the boy's hand tightens and he cries, trying to squirm out of my grasp.

"I hope she's worth it, boy," the Radical says. "Oh, I hope she's worth it."

Adam's brow furrows together in fury, his light eyes terrifying in the dark. The corner of his mouth lifts in a subtle smirk. His lips move, but I cannot hear his response. A prick of curiosity bites at the back of my mind. What did he say?

"Foolish lovesick boy," the Radical laughs. "So blinded by the heart."

Blinded by the heart? Lovesick? The need to know what he said burns all the brighter.

A broad smile stretches across Adam's face. His mouth flashes black as though he has no teeth. My mind whirls with confusion. It is not until he steps closer that I see it is not black, but blood. Adam continues forward until he is only inches away from the man. "And yet I can still see your hideous face."

Inwardly, I groan. This is not a time for your snarky remarks, Adam! I want to yell at him. The Radical swings, but Adam is ready for it. He jerks his elbow back into the Radical's stomach as he twists his wrist until the knife clatters to the floor. Both scramble for the glittering blade. Their movement is so fast, a tornado of action I cannot even begin to make sense of.

Hands reach out. Feet kick. Bodies crawl over one another. And the occasional flashing of the blade. The acidic taste of copper fills my mouth and I unclench my jaw, stopping myself from biting my tongue. I am so terribly afraid. Even more afraid than when I thought I was going to die.

The Radical's deep voice cries out and I see him slump to the side. Adam, dark bruising already forming under his left eye and blood trickling down the side of his face, slowly begins to stand. He raises his head, those eyes automatically settling on me. And my heart soars with the smallest glimpse of a smile on his bleeding lips.

The crowd quiets, the whole ship seeming to sail into a silent sphere where only Adam and I exist. We both move forward, as though pulled by some indefinite force towards one another. I stare up at him, tears welling in my eyes and sliding down my cheeks. Abruptly, his hands snap up, cupping my chin. His severe gaze travels over my face before connecting with my own. "Are you hurt?"

I fumble for a reply. His hands clamp around my shoulders, shaking me. "Are you hurt, Elvira!" he yells. I shake my head, afraid of his sudden fervor.

"Wh-what did you do to him?" I whisper.

He glances back at the Radical. "I didn't kill him."

Something pulls at my dress. I glance down to see the young boy staring up at me. Tears still line his cheeks, but his lips are utterly silent. Shame overpowers me. How could I have forgotten so easily about the child? I bend down and lift him into my arms.

"Shhh..." I comfort him. "It is all right now. No one will hurt you. It's all right."

Adam reaches out a hand to the little boy, but my eyes are peering over his shoulder. Suddenly, the Radical is behind him. Knifeless, the man slams against him and they fall back, the crowd parting as they struggle.

"Adam!" I shriek. The boy begins to cry again. "Adam!"

They inch closer and closer to the rail, a moving mass of kicks and punches. The Radical pins Adam against the three parallel bars, holding him by the neck as he connects a punch with his jaw. I scream and close my eyes, willing it to be over.

I hear them grunting as they fight. I feel the crowd watching in awe behind me.

———

A mix of shrieks and yelps suddenly forms on the lips of those around me and I know something has happened.

Unable to hide away behind closed lids forever, I open my eyes...

...Just in time to see Adam hurtling over the rail.

19
FALLING

I know what pain feels like. I know what sorrow and shame and guilt feel like, too. I know anguish. And I know fear.

But I have never known them all at once... until now. Watching Adam's body fall over the rail, each second dragged out for an eternity, I feel the pain, the sorrow, the guilt, the fear. The emotions layer on top of one another, jumbling together into a solid mass at the pit of my stomach. They escape my mouth in a piercing scream and ring in my ears. Not his name. Not a plea for help. Just tortured noise.

Unmindfully, I whip out my left hand as though reaching towards him. My heart contracts and a strange sensation like cold water rushing through my bloodstream causes me to shudder. Eyes burning and arms shaking, I grow afraid. My left wrist begins to burn like fire, the Mark seeming to glow violet even through my glove. What is happening to me?

All of a sudden, my lone scream is the only sound. Everything stills. My voice falters, allowing the silence to envelop it in its cloak. I turn to see the crowd behind me. A woman's eyes are bright with shock, ever-staring. Another has her hand raised to her mouth, frozen over her lips. A man has one foot planted on the deck, the other poised in the air as though preparing to run.

All are silent. All are frozen. Except for me and the little boy grasped in my arms.

My mind whirls for an explanation. No. My Mark is not the Mark of a... I cannot stop time... I have no powers! I have no powers! I have no powers!

I cannot think straight. The world spins around me, frozen eyes and frozen lips churning in a tornado of accusations. The colors are too bright. They blend together and blur until my eyes begin aching with the strain. Deafening quiet spills over, crashing against me with the force of a thousand orchestras. I don't understand. It seems as though the whole world is tilting, preparing to dump me off the planet alongside every lie I once believed. The biggest lie weighs me down, pulling me over the edge of the world, taking me down with it.

I have no powers. I once knew this to be true. But now it is merely a lie, dragging me down, drawing me to the ends of the earth so that I may slip away with it and disappear forever.

But no.

I will not fall with it, for if I fall, Dela will have no one. If I fall, Adam will continue to fall, too. If I fall, I will never learn the truth. And so I peel the lie away from me, allowing it to spill over the edge without me because I cannot fall. Not now. Not when Adam still hangs static over a roaring sea and certain death.

Adam!

I whip around in a flurry, rushing towards the rail. Leaning over, I see him. Doubled over and with eyes squeezed shut, he is frozen in midair. The fabric of his coat is all pulled upwards as if invisible hands hold him aloft by the cloth. I set the child down on the deck. Stepping up on the first rung, I bend over the rail and reach for his hand. I clasp my fingers around his tightly.

By the touch of my skin on his, Adam unexpectedly unfreezes. At once, my arm is jerked downwards. A cry builds on my lips as my shoulder tears away from its socket. The sudden weight hanging from my hand nearly drags me over the rail, but somehow I regain my balance. Adam's eyes are wide open now, staring up at me as his legs thrash around in the open air.

"Grab the rail with your other hand!" I yell.

His eyes grow wider and wider, but he follows my command. I pull with all my might as he scrambles up onto the rail and with one final tug, we both collapse to the deck.

Our heavy breathing coats the silence in a rhythmic

—

fog. I push myself into a sitting position and am suddenly face to face with Adam. His lips are parted as he sucks in air; his nostrils flare with the effort. But what captures my attention is his eyes. They lock onto my own, begging for an explanation I cannot give. I can see it in his expression; I can see him fighting the answer he does not want to hear. Spitting green flames, his eyes grow accusatory with each passing second.

Neither of us speaks. We just stare at one another until it becomes too much for me. The look in his eyes fills my heart with disappointment. Some part of me was clinging to the possibility that he would understand, but it was a foolish hope.

I stand and lift the little boy onto my hip with one arm. The other still throbs from the exertion. The boy no longer cries. Consumed by shock, his eyes are wide but see nothing. He is lost inside his own mind. I feel a tear slip down my cheek, but do not wipe it. With a final glance at Adam, still staring at me with that look in his eyes and no words on his lips, I turn around and slip into the crowd of statues.

My arms tingle as I try to reverse my actions. I was once told that our powers are like riding a bicycle. It comes naturally and without thought after the first time. So I close my eyes and release. Like pulling some unseen plug, I breathe life back into the world. Voices rise like an invisible wall of noise, slamming into us from all sides.

Their screams waver as they gaze down at the young man who in their minds had just fallen over the rail. Brows suddenly furrow with confusion. Heads shake in denial. Eyes blink in bewilderment.

As they yell deductions and claims of delirium, a single Marked girl rushes through the crowd with a little boy. She does not want to see the lucky young man who must have grabbed onto the rail at the last second. She does not want to stare into his eyes any longer, to see the way he looks at her now. But even as her eyes tear away from his and focus on what lies ahead, she cannot escape the memory.

His accusatory gaze still burns like green fire in the darkness of her mind, never to be extinguished.

20
TRUSTING

Blindly, I run.

Feet move beneath me, slap-slapping against the deck. A rhythmic movement that joins with my heartbeat, my breathing—everything falling into step except my racing mind.

Everything blurs, the outside world becoming a distant phantom. There is only me. Me, the little boy, and the steady pulse of running. Somewhere along the way, I run into Dela. She is still with Mr. Eversby. But even as she flails her arms around, questions bubbling out of her mouth faster than she can possibly think them, I do not stop. I just keep moving forward, knowing that they will follow. If I stop now, I may never move again. And so I keep going until without knowing how I got there, I am thrusting my way through the cabin door.

"El! Stop!" She grabs for my wrist, yanking me back. "I said, stop!" Dela's outburst is so sudden and so uncharacteristic that it jolts me. I turn to face her.

She lets out a deep breath as though cleansing herself of all anger. Well, maybe not all. "How could you run off like that at a time like this? We must flee! The whole ship is in a panic. We cannot stay with the Laurences any longer!"

"I know that!" I snap. The mere mention of his last name brings a fresh wave of pain.

"Then why are we here!"

Because this is where my mindless run took me. Because I am not yet ready to let go. Because I am sick of fleeing and hiding at any sign of trouble. There are a thousand reasons I came back, but I simply answer, "Because we need provisions."

Dela does not seem satisfied, but Mr. Eversby nods his head as he begins searching the room. "Are those real grapes on the dining table?" he says quietly to himself and shuffles off.

My sister's eyes shift. Staring over my shoulder, they widen with an unmistakable dread. Fearing the worst, I spin around on my heel.

It is Mrs. Laurence with Gertrude falling closely behind. "Oh, Miss Hamilton! Thank the heavens you are safe!" She closes the space between us with three long strides and envelops me in her warm embrace. Looking at the little boy, she says, "Oh, and who might this be?"

"I—I don't know. His mother—she—he doesn't have anybody left," I stammer.

Her eyes trace over his face, filled with sympathy. "He will stay with us," she says decisively, taking him from my arms.

My knees grow weak at her unconditional compassion. How can I possibly let go now? They weren't supposed to be here. How can I possibly leave! Dela. I can let go for Dela, I remind myself.

Mrs. Laurence sobs into my shoulder. "How could such a horrid night come to be?"

I rub her back as irritation creeps in. Who is she to cry? Am I not the one who has to flee, to leave everyone behind again? She is not the one being hunted. She does not have the shadow of death following her at every moment. And yet she cries!

"Fate," I whisper.

"No. Not fate." It is Dela speaking. I release Mrs. Laurence, turning on my sister. "This is the work of human ignorance. Nothing more," she says and shrugs. As she speaks, I do not see a twelve-year-old I must protect, but rather someone protecting me, holding me together as the world shatters.

Mrs. Laurence emits a hiccupping giggle at my sister's wisdom as she wipes at her eyes. "Oh, look at me. I am a fool. Excuse me, girls. I just fear for you both so much," she says, slipping into another fit of tears.

Gertrude offers a handkerchief. "Would you like some tea, Mrs. Laurence. It may help soothe you." I stare at her, wondering how she can possibly be thinking of tea when just outside the door, war is taking lives. No matter how hard I try to pretend otherwise, it is clear at this moment how different we truly are.

"I have found a few items that may serve useful." Mr. Eversby steps into the room—arms brimming with supplies— but comes to a stop at the sight of the two women. "Oh, dear," he whispers, summing up my thoughts exactly.

To my right, the cabin door suddenly flies open. Gertrude shrieks in surprise and Mrs. Laurence jumps. The rest of us just turn to face whatever new challenge has been presented. I peer around Mr. Eversby who stands in front of me and gasp, pulling my head back behind his cover.

Mrs. Laurence smiles at the sight that sends me into a panic. "Adam? Darling, what is wrong?"

He does not even acknowledge her. He steps into the room, slamming the door shut behind him. "Where is she?" His voice is wild, struggling in its fury to get the words out. "I said, where is she?"

"Where is who, my dear?" his mother asks innocently.
"Elvira!"

The way he drags out each syllable, every letter filled with malice, sends a bitter bug crawling beneath my skin. It is then that I begin to hate my name.

Squaring my shoulders, I step out from behind

Mr. Eversby. Adam's gaze falters, as though a hundred colliding emotions flare inside of him, but the only one I see is rage.

"You!" he spits, marching towards me. With every step he takes forward, I take one back until I am flat against the wall. "I want the truth! Tell me the truth!"

I shake my head. His anger escalates. I can feel the heat radiating from his body in waves of pure fury. Those light eyes glower down at me, seeming to darken with his mood. "Tell me!"

My bottom lip trembles as I try to get the words out, but no sound comes. He rips my arm forward, tearing my glove back. His nails scratch my skin as the glove peels away. I hold my breath and close my eyes. He makes a sound of disgust and throws my arm back down.

I open my eyes as he turns away from me, running his fingers through his thick brown hair. He paces before circling back and slamming his fist against the wall next to my head. I wince.

"You lied to me!" he yells. "I trusted you! And you lied."

"No," I say, needing him to understand. "I didn't lie!"

He laughs then, a frightening humorless laugh that scares me more than anything else. "You didn't tell the truth!"

Angry tears well in my eyes. My hands clench into fists. Is this really happening? If only I could just close my eyes and escape this moment. "How could I? I knew you would react this way. I knew if I told you, we would be handed over to the Radicals!"

Mrs. Laurence steps forward. "Oh, darling. We would never—"

"Shut up, Mother!" Adam bellows.

Her brows furrow. "Calm down this instant, son. I will not allow you to disgrace the name of this family!"

Adam whirls on her. "We've been harboring Marked! Our name is already disgraced, and you allowed it to happen!"

"You are being irrational, Adam. Elvira is—"

"One of them!" he screams. One of them? I have heard it all before, but coming out of his mouth, the words are like daggers. "She stopped time! I saw it!"

"As I recall, I saved your life!" I yell, angry at myself for ever thinking he was different. He is just like the rest of them. Ignorant and judgmental and hateful.

Dela's eyes widen, gazing at me in wonder. "You stopped time, El?"

Mr. Eversby's jaw slacks. "Impossible," he whispers.

"Impossible?" Adam laughs. "Nothing is impossible for you—you leeches!"

Mrs. Laurence gasps, cupping her hands over her mouth. Dela bows her head. Both Mr. Eversby and Gertrude look away, but I do not flinch or move my eyes away from his. Instead, I clench my jaw and hold his blistering gaze. I search for a trace of the man I thought

I knew. I search for his carefree attitude, for his sarcastic humor, for anything besides the anger and betrayal. But if it still exists, it is buried down deep within him.

"I'm sorry," I whisper.

I am sorry he cannot see past my Mark. I am sorry he turned out to be like everyone else. I am sorry I ever met him. But most of all, I am sorry I allowed him inside my heart because it only makes the pain all the more unbearable.

Mrs. Laurence stares at her son in disapproval as she grabs my arm and pulls me towards her. "Please excuse my son's insolence. I thought he was his mother's child, but it would seem he is just like his father." The way she says this I know it is a jab at Adam, and I see the way her words make him tense.

A weak smile forms on my lips and I don't know whether it is for her sake or mine. "I am sorry to have brought such unhappiness into your lives. If you will let us, we will leave and never look back," I say.

Mrs. Laurence kisses my cheek. "I will never forget you, Miss Elvira Hamilton."

Adam's lip curls with incredulity. "We need to hand them over, Mother," he says through gritted teeth.

With sudden intensity, Mrs. Laurence steps towards her son, raises her hand, and swings. The slap resonates against his cheek. My eyes widen in shock, not believing Mrs. Laurence was capable of violence. Adam gently raises a finger to his face, where an imprint of her fingers gleams in red.

"We will do no such thing," she spits. "They will escape and you will help them."

His eyes flare, but she silences him with a single finger. "She saved your life and now you will save hers. Help them onto a lifeboat. And God help you, my child, if they do not escape this ship safely..."

There is no arguing with her. She has won. I know it and Adam knows it. He shakes his head with disinclination, but steps towards the door. Embracing Mrs. Laurence one last time, I follow after him. Dela says her goodbyes and comes to stand behind me with Mr. Eversby at her side. Glancing back, I smile sadly at the woman I have come to love. She raises a hand in farewell.

"Be safe, my child. I hope we meet again," she says, a single tear wetting her cheek.

I nod. Me too, I think and step out into the hall.

Dela follows after Mr. Eversby who leads us towards the deck, peeking around corners and waving everybody on as we sneak our way to the lifeboats. Adam stomps after them, every step still weighted with his ire. The muscles in his neck and jaw are taut like wires. I trail at the back, watching him. I feel as though I am living inside a nightmare where the harder I run, the farther away he becomes. And no matter how fast I go, he is always ahead of me, standing just out of reach.

As my thoughts fill with this, he suddenly spins around to face me, blocking my path as the others continue forward. "Do you remember when we were in the bedroom and you told me about your garden?"

Bemused, I simply nod.

"And do you remember what I said? I said, 'Your secret is safe with me, Vi. Any secret of yours is safe with me. I hope you know that. I hope you know that you can trust me.'"

I cross my arms over my chest, forming a cage of steel around my heart. "Why are you telling me this, Adam?"

He sighs. "I want you to know that at that time, I meant what I said. I believed you could trust me," he says. "I'm sorry it turned out I was wrong."

Pursing my lips, I lift my chin as though his words do not affect me.

"Me too," I whisper and step by him in pursuit of the others.

21
LEAVING

"I cannot go." Mr. Eversby stands just under the lifeboat, arms crossed against his chest and his chin locked stubbornly in place.

Dela runs forward and wraps her arms around his waist. "But you must go! You simply must!"

He shakes his head. "The lifeboat needs two men to lower it. Mr. Laurence cannot do it alone. I must stay and help him."

I look up at the lifeboat, smaller than the rest but still capable of holding at least twenty passengers. On either side it is attached to the davit by chains. I silently curse the system as I search for another way. But as much as I wish and pray, there is no way around it. One of us must stay behind.

"I will stay," I whisper, but cannot be heard. I raise my voice. "I will stay!"

Adam, silent all this time, speaks up. "No."

"Excuse me? You do not get a say in this decision," I

snap. Turning to Dela, I try to explain. "My promise was to get you to America and I do not wish to break it. With Mr. Eversby you will have a better chance."

Dela wrinkles her nose in disgust. "Elvira, I do not need a sacrificial hero; I need a sister!"

I open my mouth, ready to object, but the word *sister* nags at the back of my mind. Crossing my arms over my chest, I press my lips together. You cannot leave her alone, El. She is right, my conscience tells me. I reluctantly obey it.

"Then it is settled," Mr. Eversby says. "I will stay and assist Mr. Laurence with the davits."

Not answering, I turn my head away. He takes this as acceptance and kneels down in front of Dela. She whimpers, her arms twining around him a second time. "I am sorry, Mr. Eversby," she cries. "I owe you my life."

"You owe me nothing. Only promise me that you will be safe," he says. His dark eyes lock with mine over her shoulder and he winks. I avert my gaze, unable to face leaving someone behind. This man helped me save my sister; how can I possibly abandon him to his death? The chances of him living on the ship now are slim. He will die and I will be his murderer. Just as I abandoned my parents. Just as I was too late to save the family in the kitchens or the boy's mother. His death will be on my hands for the rest of my life, but what other choice do I have?

A cold guilt clasps around me. I fight for each breath

and rush to the rail. Hanging over, I gag as though trying to throw up all of my mistakes and all of the mistakes I have yet to make. My stomach is empty and my retching produces nothing but a sore throat.

"Are you all right?"

Adam stands to my left, staring at me. Not with concern or hate, just a strange... control. It is as though he is forcing himself to hold conversation, to stand in the company of a Marked.

I wind around to face him, my anger for the night reaching its limit. "Let's not do this, Adam."

He shakes his head. "Do what?"

"Pretend!" I scream. "I am Marked. And you hate me because of it. Do not talk to me as though we don't both know this to be true. There is no point in having the company of someone who detests me. You help us escape. We forget about each other. That is all. No talking involved," I spit as my heart cries out in protest against every callous word. He may forget me, but I will never forget him. I will never forget how I felt before and I will absolutely never forget the pain I feel now.

"I wish it were that easy," he mumbles under his breath. I strain to hear him, plucking his words out of the air and attempting to string them together into coherency.

"That easy to do what?" I retort angrily.

He shakes his head and takes a step back. "I suppose it doesn't matter anymore."

"To do what?" I yell.

His features scrunch up in uncertainty and pain. "To hate you, Elvira. I wish I could hate you!"

"You do hate me!" I shriek. I pace forward. My hands raise and land on his chest, pushing at him, smacking him back against the rail with rage. "You hate me! And I hate you! I hate you, Adam Laurence! I hate you!"

He does not react. With his shoulders squared, he stares at me sadly as I pound at his chest again and again. "Fight back!" I scream. "Do something! Fight back!"

With a sudden swiftness, his hands clamp around my wrists, stopping them just before they can connect with his body. He holds them on either side of my head, the pressure almost painful. "I do not want to fight you, Elvira. I want you to get into that boat and forget about me." His eyes shift towards the lifeboat and back to me.

I cannot read his expression. His glare is stiff and neutral. Why can he not see that forgetting about him is not an option? I want to forget. Things would be so much easier if I could simply erase his memory from my mind, but life is rarely easy. Sometimes, we must remember the bad in order to remember the good.

I just wish my good and bad did not both involve Adam.

I rip my hands out of his grip and back away. Hot, angry tears burn in my eyes. I grit my teeth, shaking my head back and forth at the lunacy of it all. How have things come to be so crazy? It took only a few hours for my world to be turned upside down again.

Adam moves towards me, but I simply raise a hand. He stops. Lifting my gaze, I look him in the eyes for the last time. Hidden there in the green is something guarded. Something he cannot say and something I wish he could. A full minute passes before I open my mouth.

"I told you, Adam Laurence," I whisper. "I told you, you would not like this story."

Before he can see me break, I turn away from him and hurriedly step into the lifeboat. Dela is already sitting there, watching me with quiet concern. Mr. Eversby, holding the davits on the left, smiles at me. A goodbye. The corner of my lip somehow curves gently upward in a small smile before falling back into a frown. I do not look up again, but I feel Adam move towards the davits on the right. The lifeboat jerks as we are lowered, hitching the whole way down before the bottom just barely grazes the water.

Dela scoots towards me, placing a hand on my shoulder. "You can let go now, El." That is all she says, but it is all I need. I return to my senses, blinking as the world comes back into focus. The boat rocks softly on the water, still attached to the davits. Dela and I each detach the lifeboat from the ship as it carries us slowly away.

I look up at the monstrous ship. I think about all of the people on it. How many are Marked. How many are just caught in the middle. I think about what else the war will bring them. How many other battles will break out upon its deck. How many more balls will end in chaos. And how I will not be there. Severing the ties between the lifeboat and the *Celtic* also severed the ties between that part of my life and me. Perhaps now it will only be a small memory, tucked away behind all of the other past memories to make room for the present.

But the present is a scary thing. Dela and I are alone once again. We are surrounded by nothing but water in every direction, the ship's shadow cast down upon us, and two dark figures atop its deck left with only a few curt goodbyes.

It is as though we are looking through a glass into another world. We cannot break through, only push our faces against the cool surface and wonder if things would ever be different. If things would ever be as peaceful as the image we perceive through the glass. The ship stark against the black night, stars dotting the sky... it seems peaceful, serene, happy. You would never know someone lies dead on the deck. That a woman and three children lie cold on the kitchen floor.

Things are never as they seem. A person. A Mark. A statement. They are always deeper than we perceive, like walking in the ocean and suddenly dipping under the surface because the bottom has disappeared beneath your feet. The water appears shallow until you are suddenly flailing around beneath the surface, desperately searching for stable ground once again.

I feel myself searching for that stability now, drowning in my own confusion and guilt. I squeeze my eyes shut. Distantly, I hear yelling.

"El." My name. A barely audible whisper. "El, something's wrong." It is Dela speaking, worry lacing her voice.

The boat bobbles beneath me. "Something's happening up there, El... El!"

My eyes snap open. I look at Dela. Her golden hair hangs around her face, framing her wide blue eyes that are fixated on the ship. I follow her gaze, squinting in the dark. Four shadowy figures move hurriedly across the deck. Their yells filter down over the water. Two more shapes stand frozen near the davits, the one pushing the other away, as though telling him to run. I know who it is despite not being able to see. Mr. Eversby and Adam. The other four figures sprint towards them. One raises his hand, a gleaming metal object held out in front of him.

The bang is sudden, there and gone within a single second. It jolts Dela, but I only tense. We sit beside one another, unmoving, lips parted, eyes wide and staring. We do not dare breathe. I cannot make sense of what I am seeing until a black shape suddenly falls over the rail. A scream breaks through the night; I only realize later that it is mine. The body hits the water with a resounding splash only a few feet away from our lifeboat. A spray of water hits my face and without a moment's hesitation, both Dela and I are manning the oars, rowing towards the flailing figure.

"It's Mr. Eversby!" Dela cries.

I look again and realize she is right. He gasps for breath, thrashing around and paddling with only his right arm. Around his left shoulder, the water appears darker. The boat inches closer and finally, he gets a hand on the rim. We pull him up, the boat dipping and threatening to capsize multiple times before he finally makes it over. He collapses against the seats, his eyes fluttering shut and small puffs of air gasping through his chattering teeth. Blood mats his left sleeve, running in red watery veins across his shirt. The spot appearing redder and bigger with every passing moment.

"Oh, no. Oh, no. Oh, no," Dela chants beside me. She cups her hands on both cheeks, tears sliding through her fingers. "What will we do, El!"

I don't know. How should I know what to do? I'm only sixteen. Not a nurse. Not a mother. Only a girl. I don't know what to do! But all I say is "Start rowing."

She nods quickly as though I just gave her a very important task, and perhaps I did. The men on the deck are not happy about our rescue. I see their guns raise and take aim. I hear their yells and the firing of a gun. I feel the spray of water as bullets skid across the surface, missing us by mere inches. I look at the ship, skimming its decks for any sign of a fifth man, but see nothing. I can only hope that his absence means he escaped. As I begin tearing strips off my dress, Dela keeps rowing, taking us where a black sky meets a black sea and no light can be found.

22
PROMISING

Blood.
Everywhere.

My hands. My dress. My face.

It seems impossible for it to be covering so much of me. How did I manage to get it on my face? Did I wipe at my brow? I must have. And my neck... how did it get there? I don't understand. I don't understand any of it. My mind races. Faster. Faster. There's just so much blood. Red. Sticky. Staining my hands black in the night. Blending in with my dress.

And the screaming. Even with a ball of cloth clamped between his teeth, the screams still pierce the night in haunting waves. His eyes bulge out like a bug's and his salt and pepper hair sticks to his forehead with sweat. The boat nearly tips over with his constant spasms.

I have witnessed death before, but it was always instantaneous. Never before was there so much blood and pain and... suffering. I want to end it. I want to take away his agony, but all I can do is watch. All I can do is whisper soothing murmurings in his ear. But does he even hear them over the screaming pain?

Mr. Eversby cries out, gagging on the balled-up fabric. I cringe at the sound, pressing my hands back over the wound and trying to calm him—and perhaps myself— with meaningless chatter.

"Do you enjoy looking at the stars, Mr. Eversby?" I say in my most calming voice. Dela is crying softly behind me, grunting with the task of rowing the large lifeboat by herself. "Look over my left shoulder. Do you see the shape of a teapot? Around it are fainter stars that form the shape of Sagittarius, the Archer. Do you see him?"

I see him looking, straining past the pain into a new branch of thought. He coughs. The gag falls out of his mouth. His eyes squeeze shut and I take this as a nod.

"Sagittarius represents the centaur Chiron. You know, it is said that he was shot and wounded by Hercules. The shot brought him great agony and so he offered to switch places with Prometheus, who was being punished for giving fire to man," I tell him. I realize I am rambling. Endless prattle about unimportant matters, but I cannot stop. My mouth is beyond my control and the words keep flowing. "Chiron gave up his immortality to trade places and because of his kind act, Jupiter placed him among the stars. You can see him now, forever holding his bow and arrow."

I glance down and see him looking at me. His eyes have taken on a gentler tone, different than the intensity they once held only moments before. It is as though his mind has found a new focus, erasing the pain as he tries to make sense of the girl sitting in front of him.

"You are a brave young lady, Miss Hamilton." His words are whispers carried on the wind of short gasping breaths, but I hear the urgency laced in his speech. "You are special. You know not how much."

I can no longer fight the tears that gather. "Thank you, Mr. Eversby. Thank you for everything."

Suddenly, he grabs onto the fabric of my dress, pulling me down so that his tense eyes gaze unblinkingly into my own. "No, you must listen. You are special. My mother, she knows. She knows."

I shake my head, not understanding. Perhaps he has become delirious. "Your mother knows what, Mr. Eversby?"

His pupils grow until the dark gray of his eyes is almost impossible to discern. "You must go to her. Fifth Avenue. Elana Eversby. Fifth Avenue. Promise me. Promise, Miss Hamilton. Promise! Promise!"

Too active for his condition, he begins to choke, blood spittle dribbling down his chin and onto the white of his collar. Through the racking coughs, he continues to scream this last word at me until without knowing what I am promising, I concede.

"All right, all right, I promise!" I scream, wanting his terrifying wails to cease, for the blood to stop flying from his mouth.

Mr. Eversby becomes suddenly slack. His eyes close as though he can finally be at peace. "Fifth Avenue. Elana Eversby," he whispers. "Go to her. You promised. Go to her."

"I will. I will," I say. I squeeze my eyes shut, tears gluing my eyelashes together as I sob.

"Is he—" Dela asks from behind me. I turn to look at her. She is completely composed except for the slight tremble of her bottom lip. I feel the hot tears on my face and am ashamed. What a wild mess I must look like. I am supposed to be the strong one and I am failing miserably. I glance down at Mr. Eversby's suddenly-frozen countenance. His eyes stare unseeingly past mine, still fixated over my left shoulder.

"He is with Chiron in the stars now," I tell her.

She sniffles and nods. "He was a noble and kind friend. He deserves his place among the stars, doesn't he?"

I smile, brushing my fingers over his eyes, closing them forever. "Not even the stars are worthy of him, Dela."

We sit in silence for a moment, gazing up at the sky. I wonder how many souls I have put there. How many are now among the stars because of me. Mr. Eversby lost his life helping us escape. We have our lives because of him. Nothing I do will ever repay such a debt.

But keeping my promise may come close. I fumble over his last words in my mind. Fifth Avenue, he had said. Is that a place? A street name perhaps? Am I supposed to go there? It is impossible for me to think. Too many thoughts swim around in my head.

Needing something to do with myself, I begin to pull Mr. Eversby towards the side of the boat. His heavy dead weight is cumbersome to say the least, but I manage. The boat bobbles atop the water as I move. Mr. Eversby's lifeless body lies limp at my feet, but just as I am about to lift his leg over the edge, my sister's tiny hand clamps around my wrist.

"What are you doing?" she yells.

I turn to her, needing her to understand. "He is with the angels now. The boat is difficult to row already without extra weight. I am sorry, Dela, but it must be done."

Tears slip down her cheeks as she nods. "I know, but shouldn't we say something? A few words, maybe," she stammers.

I look at her and back at the body. I find myself wondering when I became so heartless. The idea of saying a few kind words never even crossed my mind. I have no compassion anymore, no heart. War took that from me. War took everything from me. "Go ahead, Dela."

She steps around me to sit beside him and closes her eyes. I watch her as she takes deep breaths, her light curls brushing against her cheeks.

"We did not know you for very long, Mr. Eversby, but I am glad to have met you. You saved my life more than once and you saved my sister. When we see our parents again in America, I will tell them all about you," she says.

The part about our parents makes me wince, but I do not interrupt. It is a conversation better saved for a later time. For now, I let her speak.

"I will tell them how noble you were. How kind, gentle, and good." She shudders, pausing before speaking again. "I am going to miss you. But El and I will remember you. One day, we will lie in her garden again and look at the stars. And when we do, I will think of you. Thank you, Mr. Eversby. Thank you for everything. Rest in peace."

Dela opens her eyes, glancing over at me. "How was that?" she asks.

I grin, laughing, though I know not why. "Perfect," I tell her. "It was perfect."

She presses her lips together and nods. Without speaking, we both roll Mr. Eversby up and over the side of the boat. He hits the water with a light splash before slowly slipping beneath the surface, leaving those living to face the world above alone.

"It is just you and me again," Dela says.

I pull her closer and kiss her cheek. "And we will manage just as we always have. I love you, Dela."

"I love you, too, El."

Those three words allow us to pick up the oars and

keep rowing. Those three words help us to push on. Those three words power our will to survive. Without them, we would have no cause. Without love, we would have no reason.

23
DECEIVING

Drifting aimlessly, surrounded by nothing but the same opaque blue, hunger gnawing at your stomach: these are the architects of lunacy. I feel the numbness in my mind, my humanity and intelligence dissolving into nothing... numb. Numb. Numb.

There is no thought, no feeling—only the hunger. Time is measured from one grumble of the beast to the next. My tongue feels like cotton. Chapped and swollen, my lips stick together and beg for hydration. I am surrounded by endless water and yet, have nothing to drink. Legs stick out from my body; I can see them, touch them, but I cannot feel them. Pins and needles race across my calves and thighs.

Beside me, Dela groans. The incomplete darkness of dawn surrounds us in shadows. In less than an hour, the full light of day three will shine down upon us. There is no land in sight. And the hope of spotting another form of life besides the hovering birds is dwindling fast. No. We are stranded. Lost at sea and lost in our own minds.

So lost, in fact, that when I see a dot of white on the horizon, I am sure I am hallucinating. It grows larger. Moving closer and closer, the mirage takes the form of a boat. It bobs across the water, inching closer to us. My dry and cracked throat somehow emits a laugh. It is strangled and coarse, an odd filament of noise in my ears.

Dela looks at me. She points. I follow her finger across the horizon to where my imagined boat rests atop the water.

"A boat," she says, her voice strained and foreign.

With a sudden burst of strength, I sit upright and squint into the distance. The mirage does not waver or change. Because perhaps it is not a mirage at all. Perhaps it is real! "You see it too?"

She closes her eyes and nods.

Suddenly, I am on my feet and waving my hands above my head. Cupping my hands around my mouth, I yell into the night. "Help! Over here! Help!"

Something hard slams into me, pushing me back down. The piece of wood that forms a bench digs into my side, but I cannot adjust my position due to my sister. She lies across me, her hand clamped over my mouth.

"Are you mad?" she yells at me. "They could be Radicals!"

I roll my eyes, pushing her off of me.

"Stay in this lifeboat much longer and we are dead

regardless," I spit. "I think I'll take my chances."

With a twinge of stubborn persistence in her hollow eyes, she rises and grudgingly yells across the dark expanse with me. A light plays over us and we continue to scream and wave our arms, even as the boat nears close enough for me to make out five men standing on its deck.

The boat sidles up like a grand creature hovering menacingly over our small craft. It comes to a stop parallel to us. Only a two foot gap separates us from the unknown. One of the men holding a lantern steps towards the rail of the boat and peers down at us. Most of his features are cast in shadow, the warm glow of the candlelight only falling upon his cheekbone and brow. The little of his face I can see is disguised by a thick beard. His dark eyes lock onto me and as if his initial impression wasn't enough, I am quivering with fear.

"State your name!" he barks across the small fissure between our two vessels. The sudden volume of his voice in the still night jars me. I scramble for a reply.

At last, I yell back with an unmistakable tremble in my voice, "Miss Elvira Hamilton, sir."

"And the other?" he says, gesturing with the lantern.

"My sister. Miss Dela Hamilton, sir."

He exchanges a quick glance with the other four men. My legs feel as though there is not a bone beneath my skin; the lack of food and exercise do not pair well with my sudden need for energy. I am not sure how much longer I can continue functioning.

The man turns back to me, lowering the lantern so that it casts over our faces instead. He makes an uncommitted grunt. "What is your business, Miss Hamilton?"

"We were on the RMS *Celtic* heading to America, but there was a great commotion and we were forced to escape. We've been stranded out at sea for days, sir," I say, leaving the constant lies in the past. All except one: the truth about what lies beneath our gloves.

"Which side?" he shouts.

Dela, sitting down behind me, speaks up. "I beg your pardon, sir?"

"Which side?" he repeats. "The Radicals or the Marked? Which side?"

I hesitate. Is it worth sharing the one detail I refused to share with anyone? The one verity about me I could not even bear to share with my one and only friend? *A friend you lost because you lied,* I remind myself.

I glance back at Dela who shakes her head profusely. "Don't, El," she whispers repetitively. But as wise as she is, I do not listen. Something possesses me to open my mouth and share the truth. Perhaps it is the guilt over not having told Adam. Instantly, I store that thought away. Lifting my gaze, I stare straight into the man's eyes as I say, "The Marked side, sir."

I am not sure what I expected him to do. Ram his boat into ours. Jump across the divide and latch onto my throat. Anything besides turning around and disappearing back into the boat's innards. Dela and I exchange a brief quizzical glance before I hear a faint thump. Fearing the worst, I turn to meet a harmless rope ladder dangling over the side of our sister boat, welcoming me into another chapter of the story that is Elvira Hamilton.

—

We are sitting in the captain's quarters, two men watching over us. A plate filled with a stale, hard cracker sits before Dela and me. *Hardtack*, I remember the sailors calling it. We each hold a cracker in our hands, alternating dry bites with sips of water. The metallic taste does not bother me as my stomach groans greedily. I reach for another biscuit, reminding myself to eat this one more slowly, when a woman slams through the door.

She is young, in her early twenties, and yet she does not carry the attributes I associate with most women her age. Her dark blue eyes have an element of aged wisdom in them. The skin around her mouth is devoid of laugh lines. Black hair is pulled back into a knot at the base of her neck, brushing against the collar of a once-cream workman's shirt, now tinged a faint brown. Brown trousers, black boots, and a knife concealed in her belt create the appearance of a stern sailor. Her entire persona catches me by surprise, and just when I think I have become accustomed to her attire, the man to my left speaks.

"Good evening, Captain."

I startle, wiping at the crumbs gathered around my mouth. "Captain?"

Her eyes fall down to mine. She smirks. "Captain Devry. And you must be the riffraff my boys picked up this evening."

"But you are..."

"A woman? Why, yes, I am. Happy to hear the sailor's work clothes have not completely stripped me of my true gender." She pokes a finger through a hole in her pants as though to make a point before reuniting with my hard gaze.

"We did not mean to offend you, Miss Devry. It only caught us off guard. It is so rare to find a woman in such a profession," Dela offers as she stands, making her way around the table in the center of the room. She nearly hits her head on a lantern hanging low over the work desk. Its dying flame barely lights the papers and odd contraptions strewn across the table.

"It's *Captain* Devry," she says, turning towards my sister. She looks Dela up and down, a strange look twisting her features. "How old are you, child?"

Dela looks her square in the face. "I am twelve as of this past February. If I may inquire, how old are you, *Captain* Devry?"

The woman laughs and the men join in hesitantly. Dela and I are stone silent. "You do not speak like a twelve-year-old," she says. "Nor do you act like one. The audacity it takes to ask a woman her age. Well, I cannot say I do not admire the quality." She laughs again. "I am twenty-two and I have been with this ship for five years. Captain for three. And oh how lucky you are for that good fortune. The previous Captain of The *Mermada* would have tossed you riffraff back in without a second glance."

I set my jaw, still trying to gauge how these events will unfold.

"Lucky indeed," I say dryly.

—

It takes us an hour to tell our story, from our last night in the village to floating aimlessly at sea. Skipping the more intimate details, we share what is necessary until the events of the past week are fully known. The thought catches me off guard. The past week. Is that truly all it has been? A week? It feels as though this time—this time of running and hiding—has been my entire life. As though nothing else ever existed. As though the times spent with my mother and father, happy in our home, were only dreams—something to wake up from and remember for those brief seconds before it slips away into oblivion.

Captain Devry does not make any form of

acknowledgement while we are speaking. Not a word leaves her mouth. When we finish, she only continues to stare at us, leaning back in her chair with her arms folded across her chest. Supporting her weight with only the back two legs, the chair slams back down when she leans forward again. She nods her head, as if just now absorbing all of the information.

"Let me make sure I completely understand what you are saying," she says at last. "You and your sister escaped an attack on your village by hiding away on a refugee ship heading to America. When you were discovered, you abandoned ship and somehow ended up in our good graces. And now you want passage to America where you can be free with your family?"

Dela and I exchange a brief glance. We nod.

The Captain tilts her head back and, to my astonishment, cackles. She laughs obnoxiously, tears nearly streaming from her eyes. It is strange to see a woman laugh so freely. She does not even try to hide her laughter behind a handkerchief, but rather opens her mouth to its fullest and lets her amusement loose without restraint. The men laugh too. I think back to what she said, trying to find the joke, the punchline that has clearly flown over my head, but still do not understand. Confused and afraid, I watch her in stunned silence. Dela, however, is not so quiet.

"What?" she asks shrilly. "What is so amusing?"

Captain Devry's laughter subsides into a few weak chuckles before she is able to answer. "You foolish, foolish girls!" she screams with another fit of mirth. "You left a war only to join another!" She resolves into another fit of laughter.

A sudden anger overtakes me and I fly out of my chair. "What do you mean?" I yell. "What war?"

"The Marked," she says. "The Marked and the Radicals! We are on the brink of war, my friend; America has succumbed to the madness, as well. Nowhere is safe anymore! Not for us! Not for the Marked! Oh, how foolish you are, child! You truly did not know!"

Her words race around my head in circles and I collapse back into my chair. Even with laboring breaths, not enough oxygen can gain transport to my brain. The world spins. Images of the war flash before my eyes— children lying dead on the floor, Dela barely visible through black smoke, Mr. Eversby's lifeless body floating atop the water...

I was so sure I had finally escaped it. That America would be different for us. That we would finally be treated like equals. That the war was over, at least for us.

But I was dwelling on lies.

Dela refuses to accept it. "That doesn't make sense. Why would they send refugees to America if there is a war there as well?"

I perk up. She is right; why would they?

"Because war has not yet begun. Nevertheless, it is coming. There is no doubt about it. The tension in America is at its maximum. It is only a matter of time before a real battle begins," one of the men behind me says.

Dela looks up at him incredulously. "A real battle? As opposed to what?"

Another man to my left answers. "Lynchings, knifings, skirmishes in the street. The Marked are not liked here. War has not officially broken out. But understand this, girls, the Marked are not considered equals. Not here. Not anywhere."

"But it's 'The Land of the Free,' is it not?" I argue.

The man shakes his head sadly. "Aye, it is. The Land of the Free where all men are created equal—"

"Then, I am afraid I do not understand. If all men—"

Captain Devry stands, meeting my eyes this time without humor or scorn. Instead, her gaze carries an essence of compassion and pity. "All men, my dear. The Marked are not men. The Marked are not even human."

I lean back against the table for support. She is right. They all are. I am a foolish, foolish girl. How could I ever have believed we would be treated as equals, let alone as humans! America is a lie. Freedom. Equality. It's all a lie—a pretense I was imprudent enough to believe.

"We will take you with us to America, but when we arrive, you go your way and we go ours," the Captain says.

Originally standing behind me, a man walks around

the table to face us. With grim eyes, he leans forward and says, "When you step off this ship, you will be in a war zone. Do you understand the gravity of what I just said?"

Dela looks to me. My lip quirks up in a half grin and she bites her bottom lip in return. We have an understanding. I turn back to the man with a hard glare.

"I have not seen my mother and father in a week and I do not know that I will ever see them again. I crawled into a box to be carried onto a ship with no food, no water, and no plan. I watched through a window as three children and their mother suffocated. I nearly lost my sister to the same fate. I had the blood from a fellow Marked drip from the knife of a Radical onto my face as the dead body lay next to me. I held onto a friend as the life drained from his eyes," I say, my voice rising higher and higher as I speak. "Should I go on?"

The room is dead silent. The men bow their heads, avoiding my gaze. Captain Devry stares at me coolly, a stoic charm in her eyes.

"War is in my life. It is a part of me now, whether I like it or not! So, yes, sir. To answer your question, I understand perfectly."

24
FLYING

A seagull passes overhead. Its cawing drone slices through the salty air. Closing my eyes and spreading my arms, I lean my head back and listen to the rhythmic push and pull of the ocean and the caw of the bird. The wind rushes over my face, blowing my hair out behind me. A grin breaks out upon my lips. The first one since the ball, since... Adam.

Instantly, the smile falters. My arms droop back to my sides and I open my eyes, watching as the bird performs smooth, coasting arcs across the sky. Its white feathers wink in the sunlight. I am jealous of the gull. Its ability to open its wings and jump into the sky, gliding away on pallid feathers like a ship and its sail. How easy it would be if I could just fly away whenever life got too difficult. I could forget about the war and just disappear into the sky's blue expanse.

But the closest I will ever come to the gull is this moment, standing on the bow of a ship as it flies across the water, my arms spread out like wings.

"The first gull."

The voice comes from behind me and I spin around on my heel. Captain Devry stands before me, wearing the same clothes she has for the past two days. I wear a similar outfit, finally free of the dress that only ever brought back horrid memories. As soon as I undressed, I threw it overboard, but its red beauty and the night that accompanied it still haunt my dreams.

The Captain smiles weakly and moves forward to stand beside me. We do not look at each other; instead, we both focus on the gull's sweeping dives.

"It means we are getting close," she says, inclining her head towards the bird.

"Close to where?" I scoff. "More war? More pain and suffering? That is not something I wish to get closer to."

She nods. "None of us do, but it is like you said. It is a part of us now, whether we like it or not."

I turn to her then, something she said before nagging at the back of my mind. "When you say we, Captain, are you referring to the Marked? Are you... like me?"

Smiling, she allows her eyes to finally steal away from the bird. They settle on me and I fidget under their cool gaze. "Yes, Miss Hamilton. You are not the only one upon this ship who feels the full effects of this war."

I shake my head. "But they—the crew—they treat you with such respect. They not only see you as an equal, but as a superior. How did you... I mean, how—"

She laughs. "How did I stop them from throwing me overboard at the very sight of my Mark?"

Biting my lip, I tuck my hair behind my ear. "Well, yes."

"People learn with time. They were not pleased with me when the truth was first revealed, but we were in the middle of a storm. The waves were pounding down over the deck and thrashing the ship around like a ragdoll. A strike of lightning had already taken out one of our masts. Everyone was sure that night would be the end of us all," she tells me. I hold onto her every word, her story capturing my interest and reminding me of my own life. A whirling storm I cannot escape, and me, a powerless ragdoll trapped in the gale.

She continues. "But I refused to surrender. I knew my ability could be our salvation, so I took command and steered us to safety. It still took time for them to treat me normally. But eventually, they began to see that the only differences between them and me are a Mark and an ability beneficial to any ship."

An odd jealousy crawls beneath my chest. It slithers out from a deep place I do not recognize. I am not jealous of her for her beauty or her charm or her lustrous hair. No, I am jealous of her ability to make people accept her. An ability I am clearly without. Adam could not even bear to look me in the eye, even after I saved him. But Captain

Devry? She saved her crew and they were actually grateful!

I nearly laugh aloud at the unfairness. Why could Adam not just be happy he was saved? Why did he have to look at me that way? Why? It is the question with no answers. It is the question that only leads to more questions, an endless cycle of unknowns. And it is the question that has been slashing at my heart ever since I stepped off that ship.

I ask myself that question every day, every hour, every minute. What if Adam had never found out about my Mark? What would he have said had he not been interrupted that night? I know I should stop, that the longer I allow such questions to circulate around in my mind, the longer it will take for me to let go. But it is a lost cause. I need to know.

But I will never get the chance to ask. Because he is gone and our story is over. There will be no Elvira and Adam. I am certain of it.

"Nothing is ever certain."

I emit a feeble yelp as I whirl around. Icy spiders spin webs across my back and arms, spreading chills as they weave their way through my skin. One of the crew members stands before me. He is scrawny, younger than the rest. He looks like a child despite the wispy hairs that grow in patches along his chin. His hooded eyes are a milky blue and as I shift, I realize he cannot see me. As though knowing I just realized his condition, his lip quirks up in an almost smirk; it is a painful reminder of Adam. Another wave of goose bumps nips at my arms.

"Sanders," Captain Devry scolds. "What did we talk about?"

He glowers in her direction before settling his gaze over my left shoulder. I cross my arms over my chest. Even knowing he is blind, I feel as though he can see into the deepest caverns of my soul. I squint up at his shadowy outline. The sun's rays surround him like a golden armor.

"Your friend troubles you," he says.

The hairs on my arms stand at attention, as though saluting a commanding officer. "I—I beg your pardon?"

He closes his eyes, rubbing at his temples meditatively. "In the midst of all your bothersome thoughts, he is the one constant."

"Sanders!" the Captain yells.

Horrified, I clamp my hands over my ears, as though all of my private thoughts are leaking through their openings. I look up at Captain Devry. "How does he know? How does he know what I am thinking?" I shout.

"Please," Sanders whispers. The color rushes from his face and he closes his eyes; his cheeks puff out as though he may vomit. "You are screaming inside your head. Please, stop..."

Devry puts a hand on his shoulder. "Just breathe, Sanders. Miss Hamilton, stop screaming in there."

My mouth drops open. "In where?"

"Your mind, of course. Sanders can read minds at will, but he has difficulty shutting off passionate thoughts. Evidently, your thoughts are far too emotional. Poor thing."

Her comment offends me. I am not too emotional, I think obstinately. I try to eliminate all thought, but at her words, a new set of questions comes racing through my mind. "Another Marked? How many more of us are on the ship?"

Sanders opens his eyes then. "If you divide the world into an Us and a Them, what should stop the Radicals from doing the same? We are all flesh, bone, and blood. We are all one."

The Captain rolls her eyes. "Sanders and I are the only two Marked crew members. He lost his eyesight in a skirmish with a Radical about a year ago; he somehow found his way onto our ship and we kept him. Lucky bastard!"

A small part of me still flinches at her crude language.

"It is you who is lucky," Sanders says and laughs.

I stand in silence, observing the two, but not participating in conversation until I am called upon.

"Miss Hamilton, you never did tell us, what is your gift?" Captain Devry suddenly asks.

I open my mouth, unsure as to how to answer, when Sanders speaks for me.

"The girl can tell you no better than that seagull

floating overhead. The Mark does not match the one power she exhibited and even that, she questions."

My cheeks grow hot with shame, though I know not why. Irritation helps fuel the blood rushing to my face. My every thought is a grand magic lantern show for his amusement, a never-ending stream of entertainment.

"There is no amusement in hearing one's thoughts," he spits. His abrupt vehemence terrifies me. "Amidst the riveting gossip and few humorous fancies, there is also the deception and wickedness of man that I play witness to every day. People are cruel beings and all have a dark side, Miss Hamilton. Do not let the exterior fool you. The mind tells all."

Oh, really? I think. If the mind tells all, can it tell me what Adam truly feels? Can it tell me why I cannot stop thinking about him? Can it tell me why, amidst all of the cruel glares I have received throughout the years, his hurt so much more? If the mind tells all, tell me that!

My eyes widen as I realize those private thoughts are not so private anymore. I cringe, my nose wrinkling with regret.

"I'm sorry," I mumble. Captain Devry looks at me, clearly confused, but Sanders just smiles. His teeth are yellowed, crooked at odd angles.

He straightens from his hunched posture, tucking his hands into his pockets. "It is quite all right. I best be returning to my duties or else I will be in trouble with the

Captain." Another Adam-like smirk twitches at his lips. My gut churns. Reaching out a hand, his fingers feel the air for a moment before finally locking onto my shoulder. He leans forward to whisper in my ear, "As for your question, perhaps your mind cannot tell you because only your heart knows the answer."

Riding on the stench of his breath, the profound words he speaks seem out of place coming from his lips. However, I refuse to acknowledge the truth in his remark. Adam does not hold a place in my heart and soon, he will not hold a place in my mind either. Some way or another, I will let go.

His vacant, opaque eyes constrict, but he does not refute my reflection. Nodding to the Captain and me, Sanders leisurely saunters off.

The Captain turns to the rail, leaning her head back and allowing the warm sun to light her cheeks. "Sanders is quite the character, is he not?"

"He certainly is," I agree. With a sigh, I rest my arms along the bars of the handrail and look into the sky. The bird still coasts in even circles, though its small form is distant. I can no longer make out the black tips of his feathers nor his yellowing underbelly.

"Miss Hamilton, when Sanders said you do not know your abilities any more than the bird circling in the sky, what did he mean?"

I shrug. "Up until a few days ago, I was sure I had no

powers," I say.

"And now?"

With a sigh, I say, "And now, I have an ability, but no explanation. The Mark on my wrist cannot stop time and yet, I can. Sanders was right; I am as clueless as the gull."

The Captain glances at me from the corner of her eye. "Do you believe you will find the answers in America?"

I smile, remembering Mr. Eversby's last words to me. *You are special. You know not how much.* And with this memory comes the recollection of the promise I made to him. "I do not know," I reply. "But an old friend believes I will. And I have every faith in him."

Turning to face me, Captain Devry smiles, two small dimples pinching into her cheeks. "Well, Miss Hamilton, let us see if your friend was right." Her grin broadens until her teeth are visible, glistening with zeal. She moves behind me, placing her hands on my shoulders. She leans forward to speak into my ear, giving my shoulder one last gentle squeeze before walking away. "Take a look at the horizon," she says.

Squinting past the glimmering dust and shining sea, both alight with the sun's beams, I gasp at the sight. Glinting like silver daggers jutting out over the face of the water, the luminescent steel of newly-built skyscrapers flashes. Another bird flits overhead, joining The *Mermada* in its journey to this new world. The American dream rests before me in a blend of steel, innovation, and endless possibilities. My future rests atop its sharp angled buildings, in its beautifully corrupt walls and the secrets that lie in the fading brick.

The secrets I will come to learn.

And the secrets I will one day leave behind.

About the Author

Kelseyleigh Reber lives in Pennsylvania with her family where her favorite room remains her bedroom-turned-library. Having loved reading and creating the written word since she was a small girl, Kelseyleigh is a self-professed bibliophile with a passion for both the fantastical and historical. She also has a strong passion for chocolate, but that book has yet to be written.

CPSIA information can be obtained at www.ICGtesting.com
Printed in the USA
OW04s1403140813

572BV00001B/3/P